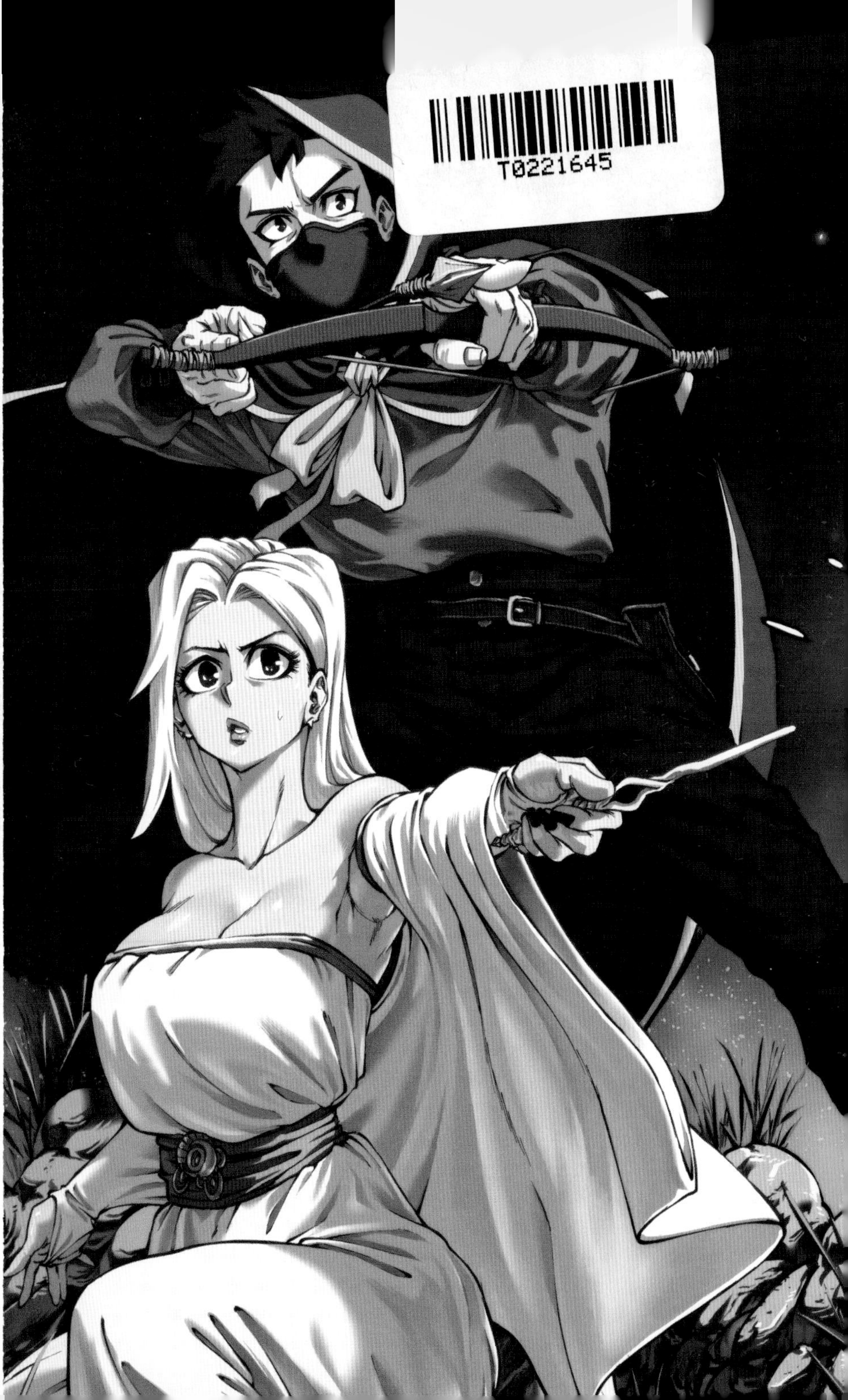

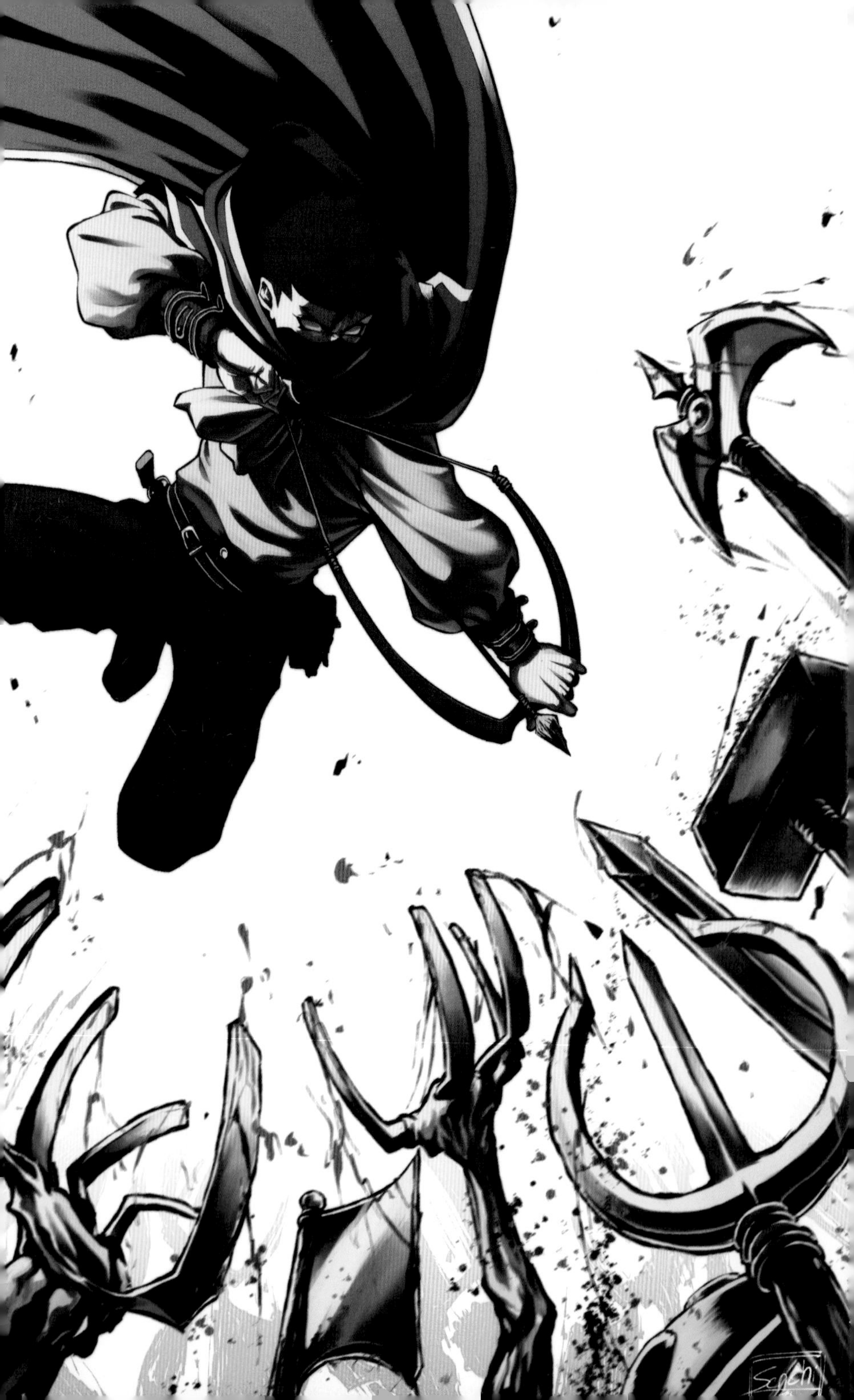

THE PRIMAL HUNTER

VOLUME 1

WRITTEN BY
ZOGARTH

ILLUSTRATED BY
SENCHIRO

vault

VOLUME 1

WRITTEN BY
ZOGARTH

ILLUSTRATED BY
SENCHIRO

AETHON
BOOKS

vault

EDITORIAL
ADRIAN WASSEL — CCO & EDITOR-IN-CHIEF
DER-SHING HELMER — MANAGING EDITOR
DESIGN & PRODUCTION
TIM DANIEL — EVP, DESIGN & PRODUCTION
ADAM CAHOON — SENIOR DESIGNER & PRODUCTION ASSOCIATE
NATHAN GOODEN — CO-FOUNDER & SENIOR ARTIST
SALES & MARKETING
DAVID DISSANAYAKE — VP, SALES & MARKETING
SYNDEE BARWICK — DIRECTOR, BOOK MARKET SALES
BRITTA BUESCHER — DIRECTOR, SOCIAL MEDIA
OPERATIONS & STRATEGY
DAMIAN WASSEL — CEO & PUBLISHER
CHRIS KANALEY — CSO
F.J. DESANTO — HEAD OF FILM & TV

TABLE of CONTENTS

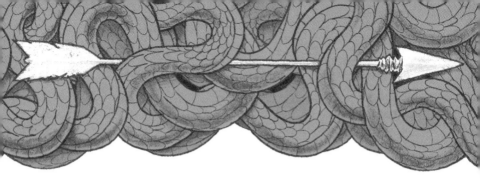

CHAPTER 1
ANOTHER MONDAY MORNING

It was just another boring Monday morning. The sparse rays of sunlight that found their way through the blinds' narrow gaps did little to disturb the man sleeping deeply on the bed. However, the serene peace was short-lived as the accursed sound of his alarm began its daily ritual of ruining a good dream.

Jake, who had previously been enjoying the sweet embrace of his blankets, was startled awake, fumbling around until his hand finally found his phone. Grumbling, he rolled out of bed and started his usual morning routine, preparing for yet another day at work.

He went for a warm shower, ate a quick breakfast, and got himself dressed before he finally grabbed his stuff and headed out the door. The entire morning routine was done in less than half an hour.

Walking down the stairs to his car, he had an intuition that the day was going to be interesting. He didn't know why, as everything was as usual so far, but he couldn't entirely dispel the feeling. *Maybe someone brought donuts?*

Traffic was terrible as usual, living in a big city and all. He spent most of the time not actually driving but sitting in the endless queues of the morning rush. He had considered cycling or maybe running to work, but then he would have to shower and get dressed at work, and that just sounded bothersome.

As he finally pulled into the parking lot, he got out, grabbed his bag, and headed inside the corporate office that had been his workplace for the last couple of years. The building itself was a massive monstrosity of glass, with way too many floors. It wasn't all that out of place, though, being surrounded by similar structures.

As he got inside, he was greeted by the receptionist, Joanna. She was a middle-aged woman, one who always wore these large earrings and more makeup than an entire class of high school girls would need in a week. If Jake had to describe Joanna in the easiest way possible, it would be a soccer-mom stuck in a perpetual mid-life crisis. The reception was located only a couple of meters away from the elevators, so greeting her in the morning was a natural routine for most employees.

"Morning, Jake, had a good weekend?" she asked with far too much energy for this early in the morning.

"Same as always, how about you?" Jake answered politely, knowing what was to come.

"Oh, it was great! You know, me and Mike tried to..." She explained with vigor and in great detail, giving Jake déjà-vu to last week, where the exact same scenario seemed to have played out.

After the far-too-long conversation about inane subjects with her, the arrival of the elevator finally saved him, allowing his escape as he headed up to the fourteenth floor.

Stepping out of the elevator, Jake was met by a calm, open-office space. *Seems like I am one of the first to arrive today*, he thought as he found his way to his desk. Booting up the computer, he started going through the emails that had come during the weekend.

Jake had worked in this office for a bit over two years now. His job was what many would describe as boring, yet he somehow found it peaceful to immerse himself in the spreadsheets, financial reports, and whatnot. He worked in the financial department, and if he said so himself, he was rather good at what he did.

He mainly worked with investments, his official title being a business analyst. Jake had a knack for picking out the excellent stocks and avoiding the bad ones. He had always had a good gut feeling about those kinds of things.

The office slowly got filled up as more and more employees made their way off the elevator. After the initial morning greetings and polite social exchanges, the noise slowly died down and everyone got busy with their respective tasks. *No donuts,* he noted internally with great disappointment.

As he sat there, having finished up the most immediate tasks, he began to feel a bit tired once more, clearly having not gotten enough sleep. Most others in the office had learned by now that he wasn't one for small talk, so most left him alone. Just the way he wanted it.

Jake had always been a rather laid-back person, cautious and a bit withdrawn. He had always been a bit of a loner and chosen activities based on not interacting with others. Heck, when his dad had forced him into doing some kind of sport to get him out of his room, he'd chosen archery, as he could do that entirely on his own.

All in all, Jake was content with his life. He had a well-paying job, a good family, a nice apartment, and great colleagues, and his future was looking bright, if he said so himself. He wasn't an extraordinary person, but just another face in the crowd. And he kind of liked it that way.

Standing out meant unnecessary attention, and he preferred to avoid that.

As he finished his thoughts, his supervisor, Jacob, walked over with a big smile on his face.

"Hey there, buddy! Me and the others are heading out for lunch. You wanna come?"

"Eh, sure, sounds good," Jake replied tentatively.

He liked Jacob. Jacob was the kind of guy that people would call a born leader. Excellent social skills, with an affinity for reading people and making them feel comfortable around him. He was one of the few people that Jake called a friend.

Following him was a guy called Bertram. Big and brooding would be one's first assumption, but he was actually a big softie. Apparently, he had taken care of Jacob while growing up and was akin to a butler or something.

All he knew was that Jacob's family was filthy rich. It was quite honestly a miracle that Jacob hadn't turned out to be an entitled brat instead of the man he was today. He was popular in the office by every metric, especially with a *certain* clientele.

His handsome looks, tall stature, and overall charm certainly did him no harm when it came to the women in the office. His hair always seemed to sit with impossible perfection, his suit was always worn perfectly, and what seemed like an eternally relaxed smile adorned his face.

They managed to get along mainly due to the man's ability to carry a conversation longer than a few sentences, even with someone like Jake. The fact that Jake wasn't the type to create problems in the office, but only deliver reliable results, naturally only made their relationship easier for both sides.

Which was also the reason why Jake agreed to go to lunch. Because with Jacob along, he knew it wouldn't be entirely awkward.

Jake got up and made his way to the elevator together with Jacob and Bertram, talking along the way about work and the meeting they had planned for after the lunch break.

He spotted Joanna and Mike, her husband, getting into the same elevator that he, Jacob, and Bertram were heading into. Said elevator quickly got cramped, as three others were already in the elevator waiting to go down—one of these three being Caroline.

Caroline was a coworker from the human resources department, who shared their office space with Jake's department. She was a year younger than him, slim, blonde, and quite frankly everything that Jake would refer to as "his type."

He was aware that this was likely just due to her being one of the only women around his age that he interacted with regularly. Just two people of the opposite sex in close proximity. Which was one of the reasons he never acted on the emotion. Along with quite a few others. He wasn't really the romantic type, and his prior experience in romance hadn't exactly panned out. *Well,* he thought, *her cheating on me with my best friend does count as "not panning out," right?*

Thus, he only managed to give her a nod and a small "good morning," despite it being noon. Jake was barely able to hold his embarrassment back from showing, but luckily, she appeared to just take it as a bad joke.

Jake was perfectly aware that Caroline barely saw him as a friend and had no romantic interest in him whatsoever. Jacob, on the other hand, she clearly had her eyes on. Not that Jake could blame her. Jacob was a great dude, no matter how you put it, and he could simply not bring himself to dislike the man, despite him being Jake's unaware, one-sided rival in love.

Jake himself was what one would describe as rather average in the looks department. Not too fat, not too slim, short brown hair, brown eyes, and a face that couldn't be described as handsome or ugly.

The only thing he had going for him was his above-average physique, mainly stemming from him still doing archery for fun in his free time, even having a homemade practice range at his parents' place. This, coupled with his gym membership (which he actually used), had let him maintain his healthy lifestyle since the time he'd still dreamed of being an athlete.

DING!

The sound of the elevator closing quickly brought him back to reality, and the descent toward the ground level began. And just as his thoughts began to wander toward what to get for lunch, his thought process was interrupted once again.

> *DING!*

A sound eerily similar to the elevator filled his head, while, simultaneously, words appeared before his eyes—in his mind, rather. He barely managed to make them out before he blacked out.

> *Initiation of the 93rd Universe confirmed.
> Introduction and tutorial sequence
> commencing*

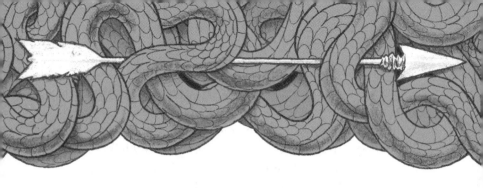

CHAPTER 2
INTRODUCTION

> *Initiation of the 93rd Universe confirmed.
> Introduction sequence commencing*
> *Welcome to the introduction. Preparing...*

As Jake opened his eyes, he was greeted by the voice once again welcoming him to an... introduction? And something was preparing? What the hell was going on?

Several seconds passed, and despite his eyes being open, he saw only complete darkness. His body felt numb all over, and the only thing he could feel was a creeping headache. He tried opening his mouth to no avail, as he started panicking internally. Had he been kidnapped by aliens? As his thoughts started to spiral, the voice suddenly sounded out again.

> *Preparations complete. Starting introduction*

Light filled his eyes as he was temporarily blinded by what seemed like a huge spotlight shining in his face. As his eyes slowly adjusted, the feeling in his limbs returned. He found himself looking down at his legs, noticing himself sitting in a chair. As he slowly looked up, he found someone sitting across from him with a table placed in between.

The room itself reminded Jake of an interrogation room, with the two chairs and a table in a small, closed-in space. All it lacked was a two-way window. The other difference was how perfectly clean everything was. The walls and floor were white, the table white, the chairs white, and despite there being no apparent light source, the whole room was somehow still well-lit.

"Hello?" Jake cautiously asked the... person across from him.

He/she looked human at a glance but had no discernible features. A bald head, completely white eyes with no pupils, and a chest that looked far too flat and undetailed to be natural. Not a single speck of hair could be seen on the body, and despite him being unable to confirm due to the table, he had a creeping suspicion this... thing didn't have anything "down there" either. As his internal assessment was finishing up, the "human" opened its mouth.

"Greetings, human. I oversee your introduction," the thing said in a synthetic voice that resembled a bunch of male and female voices mashed together. "In this introduction, I shall explain to you the circumstances of your new reality."

As Jake was about to open his mouth to respond, it started talking again.

"First of all, allow me to welcome you to this new chapter of your life. Your universe has finally passed the minimum threshold required to enter the multiverse and has thus been initiated. Now, do you have any questions before we move on to the subjects pertaining to the tutorial?"

Jake's mind was in turmoil. Multiverses? What threshold was passed? And what did it mean with a new chapter? But instead of posing any of these actually meaningful questions, he asked the most mundane thing possible:

"Who—no, what—are you?" he blurted out, stumbling over his words.

"I am the entity in charge of greeting you and introducing you to the new world, and the circumstances of your new reality."

"What new reality?" Jake asked.

"The reality named by the first enlightened races as 'The System.'"

"How do I see this sys—" Before he managed to finish his words, a screen suddenly appeared before his eyes:

Status
Name: Jake Thayne
Race: [Human (G) – lvl 0]
Class: N/A
Profession: N/A
Health Points (HP): 90/90
Mana Points (MP): 80/80
Stamina: 70/70
Stats
Strength: 7
Agility: 8
Endurance: 7
Vitality: 9
Toughness: 7
Wisdom: 8
Intelligence: 8
Perception: 10
Willpower: 6
Free Points: 0

Titles
N/A

Well, that answers that question, Jake thought. He was starting to form an idea in his mind of what was going on and decided to just roll with it. He was kind of under the impression that this was likely just a weird lucid dream, so he saw no reason not to entertain himself a bit. So, first of all, he did what he thought was fun and started analyzing the stats.

So, nine different stats, ranging from 6-10 points in each... His stats were very balanced, with only Willpower and Perception being stand-outs. Did Willpower being only at 6 indicate that he had a weak will? Was 6 low for someone in his situation?

His race said human, that part being quite self-explanatory, but what did the "G" mean? And he was apparently a level 0 human. He seemed to have neither a class nor a profession. Though he would argue himself to be upper-middle class, with his profession being a financial consultant, he doubted that was what the system meant with those two.

No titles either, and health and mana being at 90 and 80, respectively, led to his assumption that they were based on one of his stats, by a factor of 10. Vitality, being the only stat at 9, led him to conclude that it was the stat determining health. Mana was a bit more difficult, being at 80, with both Wisdom and Intelligence at 8, one of those two likely determining factors. Stamina was at 70, which, following his prior deduction, meant it was either linked to Strength or Endurance, Endurance being the stat on which he would put his money.

He tried to focus on the different elements on the screen, seemingly to no avail. It simply informed him that Strength meant Strength, and that class meant class... As he tried to focus on his race, however, it did yield a result:

> **Human (G)** – The lowest level of humans in the system. This type is found only in newly initiated worlds. The human race is known as one of the most balanced and numerous amongst the myriad races of the multiverse, being able to walk many different roads on their path to power. Stat bonuses per level: +1 to all stats. +1 Free Point.

Thanks for calling me the lowest level of human, I guess? Jake thought. The description does kind of confirm more races being out there, and also that more humans exist out there in what that thing called the multiverse.

He fiddled a bit more with the menu, trying out pretty much everything he could before he looked up at the weird human-like thing again.

"Hey, can I ask about the different stats on the status screen and their effect?" he asked. "Such as what different stats are linked to health points, or if there is a link at all?"

"No. It tells you what you need to know for now."

"May I ask how I am supposed to get a class and profession? It mentions a level here; how do I level up? What does the 'G' after my race mean? Also, why am I here to begin with? Where did the others go?" His questions came off a bit overbearing. Not that he blamed himself—this situation was without a doubt the most bizarre he had ever experienced.

"Your class is chosen upon entering the tutorial. This class shall be the starting point of your journey and help guide your path. A profession becomes available through performing associated tasks with said profession, either for a long enough period of time or through competence in said tasks. Classes are focused on the pursuit of Strength, while professions are the path of creativity, rarely offering direct increases in Strength. You level up through a wide variety of actions. The 'G' after your race states the current rank of your race. You are here because you entered the introduction. By 'others,' I shall deduce that you mean other earthlings. Said other earthlings are now also in their own respective introductions." Its explanation was concise, not giving much detail, but at least giving Jake a far better idea what was going on. It was especially good to know that his coworkers were relatively fine and likely in a similar situation as him.

"Now, on to classes," the thing said, unprompted.

Before he could even open his mouth, he was interrupted by a screen appearing before him, showing quite a wall of text. He quickly collected himself and started going through the classes one by one:

> **Warrior (Light) – Basic starting class. A light-class warrior focused on quick attacks, evasion, and finesse. While faster than both the medium and heavy variants, it comes with a decrease in attack power and survivability. Mainly uses weapons such as rapiers, daggers, small hatchets, and throwing weapons. Stat bonuses: +2 Agi, +1 End, +1 Str, +1 Vit, +1 Free Point.**

The first class appeared to be a light-class warrior, perhaps something like a rogue? It did mention both daggers and throwing weapons. This appealed to him slightly, though he was quite reluctant to be the guy fighting up close and personal. He had chosen archery and not fencing, after all.

> **Warrior (Medium) – Basic starting class. A medium-class warrior, focused on a balanced approach to combat, finding a**

compromise between speed and power. While faster than the heavy variant, it is slower than the light-class warriors. While survivability and power are higher than the light-class variant, it is lower than the heavy-class warriors. Able to use a vast array of weapons of both the heavy and light variants. Stat bonuses per level: +1 Agi, +1 End, +1 Vit, +1 Str +1 Tough, +1 Free Point.

The second one looked like the choice one would make if they wanted to be a warrior but were clueless about which direction to specialize in. Though perhaps it did provide some versatility.

Warrior (Heavy) – Basic starting class. A heavy-class warrior, focused on power and survivability while sacrificing speed and variance. The heavy warrior is slower, with a less varied approach than both the light and medium class, but in turn, gains great power and survivability. Mainly uses a combo of one-handed weapons and a shield or a two-handed weapon. Generally lacking solid ranged options. Stat bonuses per level: +2 Str, +1 Tough, +1 Vit, +1 End, +1 Free Point.

The beefy-boy option of the warrior archetype. Big and heavy, in his mind wearing full plate armor and a huge tower shield. Or maybe a super muscular, bare-chested, bearded Viking with a huge axe? Yeah, he couldn't see himself being either of those.

Archer – Basic starting class. A class focused on ranged combat, mainly using bow and arrow, coupled with light options for melee such as shortswords and daggers. The class is fast and flexible, focusing on Agility over Strength. Stat bonuses per level: +2 Per, +1 Agi, +1 End, +1 Str, +1 Free Point.

Well, here we go. Without any surprises further down the list, this seemed like the most appealing choice by far. Disregarding the light options for melee, if he had to fight in any way—which he had a strong suspicion he would have to—he would, without a doubt, prefer to do so with a bow.

Caster – Basic starting class. The caster is focused on magical combat, favoring wisdom and knowledge over brawn and speed. The basic class is non-attuned, meaning not yet specialized in any element or type of magic, thus limited in power but wide in scope. Casters wield powerful destructive abilities, though often lack in defensive options. The class mainly uses catalysts such as staves, idols, relics, or wands in order to amplify the power of magic. Stat bonuses per level: +2 Int, +1 Wis, +1 Will, +1 Per, +1 Free Point.

Well this, if not everything before it, confirmed magic being a real thing. While the concept of being a fire-flinging, lightning-bending badass did sound appealing, he would honestly prefer to just have a bow.

Healer – Basic starting class. The healer can mend injuries, remove afflictions, and amplify the power of themselves and/or their comrades. The basic class is non-attuned, meaning not yet specialized in any deific powers or types of magic, thus limited in

> power but wide in scope. The class is weak in solo combat, lacking offensive options, but powerful when surrounded by allies. Stat bonuses per level: +2 Will, +2 Wis, +1 Int, +1 Free Point.

And the last option seemed to be a healer. All classes were "basic starting classes," meaning no special overpowered starting classes. At least not for him. He also noted that all classes provided a total stat boost of 5 per level and one Free Point. Compared to race, classes seemed to offer more specialized stats, but less overall, though that may have just been due to him being human. The healer class did not appeal to him at all, though it did have quite an interesting line about deific powers. Did this imply the existence of gods? Could one become a priest of some kind down the line, perhaps?

"Hey, can you tell me anything more about these classes?" Jake asked, hopeful. "Any advice or tips?"

"Your path is for you to discover. Now choose a class before we proceed."

Realizing he may as well pick the class he'd planned on all along, Jake chose the Archer class.

> You have chosen the Archer class. Confirm?

Looks like even the mighty system is prone to security prompts like these, Jake thought as he affirmed the decision.

> *You have obtained the Archer class*

As soon as those words appeared before his eyes, he felt a weird tingling in his head, neither unpleasant nor comfortable. At the same time, some items appeared on the table in front of him. Before he had any chance to look at them further, he was once again greeted by several system messages:

Gained Skill: [Basic Archery (Inferior)] – An Archer's best friend is the bow in his hand, and the arrow in his foe's heart. Unlocks basic proficiency with bows, crossbows, and adds a minuscule bonus to the effect of Agility and Strength when using a ranged weapon.

Gained Skill: [Basic One-Handed Weapon (Inferior)] – The Archer may not be a master in the arts of close combat but is far from helpless. Unlocks basic proficiency with most one-handed weapons and adds a minuscule bonus to the effect of Agility and Strength when using a fitting melee weapon.

Gained Skill: [Archer's Eye (Common)] – The eyes of the Archer are trained to track down and spot the weakness of their foes. Allows the Archer to more easily spot prey. Passively gives a minor increase to the effect of Perception on visual organs.

As he read through the three messages, his suspicions of this new system being extremely similar to videogames or perhaps tabletop RPGs was once again confirmed. All three seemed rather basic, especially the two skills that literally had "basic" in their names. Both were only "inferior" in what he assumed to be their rank. The last one seemed a bit more interesting, being less basic and even considered a common-rarity skill.

Furthermore, he instinctively knew how Archer's Eye worked. He tried to focus and suddenly felt his vision become far clearer than it had been before. It was like he gradually switched from low quality to full HD in around five seconds or so as he focused. He looked around, enamored with how distinct everything appeared. As he deactivated the ability, and his vision returned to normal, he looked at his resources and saw that stamina had dropped from 70 to 68, with mana and health both remaining maxed out.

He closed the window and looked toward the items on the table. He looked at the thing sitting eerily still, and inquired, "I assume these things are for me?"

"Yes," it answered. "They are basic starting equipment based on your starting class. Now, on to the final step of the introduction. Some necessities are given to all new initiates of the system."

And as it finished those words, Jake was once again greeted by a screen appearing before him.

> *Gained skill*: [Identify (Inferior)] – Basic identification skill, known by all but the smallest of children of the myriad races. The skill allows you to attempt to identify any object or creature you are focusing on.

A skill that would actually allow him to get some semblance of information, maybe? Something he felt like he severely needed. Only more and more questions kept appearing throughout this entire introduction ordeal, with little to no answers.

"The time allotted for the introduction is coming to an end in ten minutes, and you will be transported to the tutorial," the thing said. "It is recommended to acquire the equipment given before the end of the introduction, or the items will be lost."

Jake panicked slightly as he went up to grab the stuff on the table.

The items included a bow and quiver, a brown cloak, a knife, and a small satchel attached to a belt. They all looked rather medieval, the bow being wooden compared to the modern compound bows he was used to, which were normally made of aluminum and other modern composite materials. The string itself was made of what seemed like silk, perhaps. He was honestly unsure.

The cloak was from a rather coarse material, reminding him of burlap, but it seemed quite durable. The quiver was made of wood with leather spun around it, and a leather harness to wear it on the back.

The knife seemed to be as simple as they come and was just a steel blade attached to a wooden handle. The quality of all the items was rather good, in his opinion. Last but not least, he looked at the small satchel and, upon opening it, found a couple of small bottles.

As he wondered what they were, he nearly slapped himself across the head, remembering his identification skill. He started focusing on one of the bottles containing red-tinged liquid, and after three or four seconds, a new screen appeared:

> [Health Potion (Inferior)] – Restores health when consumed.

What did he expect? As simple as they come. He used Identify on the other items in the satchel one by one, finding a total of three health potions and three stamina potions, which did the exact same thing as the health potion, but for stamina. As he closed the satchel, he moved on to the other items. The bow, knife, and cloak yielded no results, simply informing him that the wooden bow was a wooden bow and that the brown cloak was a brown cloak. With little hope, he inspected the quiver, and was positively surprised:

> [Enchanted Quiver (Common)] – A quiver enchanted with the ability to conjure common-rarity arrows when injected with mana.

That sure as hell seems useful, Jake thought. As he was finishing up his inspection, he was once more kindly reminded that he did not have infinite time.

"Two minutes until the start of the tutorial."

Jake, in a rush, got the cloak over his head, started attaching the belt with the satchel on it, and threw the quiver over his shoulder. Luckily, it already had dozens of arrows in it. The belt also came with a small sheath, which he promptly placed the knife in, and closed the small leather buckle meant to keep it in place. Finally, he took the bow in his hand, having no obvious place to attach it to his person. After a bit of thinking, he put it over his shoulder and stood ready for whatever was to come.

"Ten seconds to the start of the tutorial," the humanoid thing reminded him.

"It was nice to meet you, I guess, whatever you are," he said as he waved it goodbye. He was a bit afraid, but more so than that, he felt a small sense of excitement build up in the pit of his stomach.

> *Introduction sequence completed. Transporting to tutorial...*

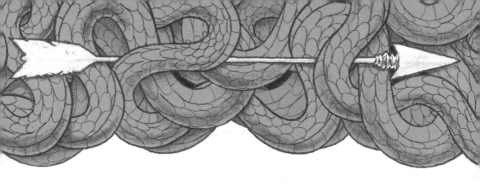

CHAPTER 3
THE TUTORIAL COMMENCES

Jake felt as though he'd simply blinked his eyes and then suddenly found himself somewhere entirely different. There was no prompt except the system message, no feeling of being thrown through time and space; he just kind of... moved.

He found himself in a... room? This one was far larger than the one before. Scratch that—calling it a room was a bloody understatement. Despite him being able to see the ceiling, he could only barely make out what seemed like a wall far off in the distance to one of the sides. On the roof was a huge circular light that appeared to act as a sun.

Looking from the ceiling to the wall, this entire place seemed to have some kind of circular design, like a huge dome. He was standing on what he could only identify as a huge pillar, one of many that were spread in all directions.

Where one would expect the floor to be, he instead saw a vast forest spreading out in all directions. Yet none of the trees even reached close to the top of the pillar. Not due to the trees being small—some looked easily over a hundred meters tall—but due to the pillar being so monstrously tall itself.

As he was starting to wonder if the system had somehow forgotten him or what exactly was happening, the trusty window and voice appeared again.

> *Welcome to the tutorial*

He felt a warm glow in his entire body as he heard the sound of yet another accompanying notification.

> Title earned: [Forerunner of the New World]

A title? One that I assume everyone gets, Jake thought, quickly checking it out.

> [Forerunner of the New World] – Complete the introduction and enter the tutorial as a forerunner of the New World. +3 all stats. Grants the skill: [Endless Tongues of the Myriad Races (Unique)].

+3 to all stats out of nowhere could only be welcome. Likely also the source of the warm glow from before. Though he still was far from sure exactly how much that would help. The skill, however, was a bit more tangible as he looked at what it did.

> [Endless Tongues of the Myriad Races (Unique)] - Allows you to communicate with the myriad races throughout the multiverse. A unique skill granted for free to the forerunners of a newly initiated race.

The skill somehow allowed him to communicate with other races. Was it only speech, or writing too? Again, more questions, and attempting to focus on the skills yielded no further results. He even attempted to use his newly acquired Identify skill, though nothing happened.

Hearing something behind him, he was startled and quickly turned around to find that someone else had been transported to the same platform. With a hand on his knife handle, he noticed who it was.

"Jacob?" he asked rhetorically, looking at the man before him. Jacob was no longer wearing his suit, but was instead donning chainmail, gauntlets, and what looked like leather pants with a pair of sturdy-looking boots. The entire thing looked like it had been taken out of the costume rack from a medieval movie.

Jacob also appeared flummoxed by the entire situation as he took a second or two to collect himself before hearing and seeing Jake.

"Jake!? Oh, man, is it good to see you! Have you seen any of the others?" Jacob spoke with his usual high energy in a hopeful voice.

"Nah, I am just as surprised to see you here. After we entered the elevator, did you also—»

But before Jake had a chance to ask, another flash of light appeared, and yet again—before he could even see who it was—another flash of light, and then another, until there were a total of ten people on the platform.

Jake instantly recognized all the people, as five of them had been in the elevator with him, and another four were other employees at his company. To his relief, Caroline was amongst the new arrivals and looked to be fine, now donning a white robe with what looked like a small wand at her hip.

"What happen—»

"Hey, why—»

"You seen Mike!?"

"Where is—»

Everyone began speaking over each other; all confused, but some more than others. Jake simply stood back as he tried to internally grasp the situation while, of course, listening to the others. After the initial panic had settled, they all calmed down and began assessing their situation. They were all professionals, after all. It had nothing to do with Jacob trying to calm them. Not at all.

After a quick round of questions and answers, it seemed like they had all been transported to their own respective interrogation-like room and had gone through roughly the same ordeal as Jake had. However, Jake did learn that he had apparently missed some questions, as the others had discovered a few more details. One of which was that new skills could be earned every five levels with their classes.

As they moved on, they also did a tally on their different classes. They turned out to have one light, two medium, and one heavy-variant warrior, two archers, three casters, and one healer. Rather balanced—something Jake suspected the system had done on purpose. Or maybe just luck.

Their armor and outfits also greatly differed. They were no longer all wearing their nice dress shirts and "presentable" clothes. The light warrior had leather armor; medium warriors—Jacob being one of them—had a set of chainmail; and the heavy warrior wore what looked like rather poorly made iron armor.

The other archer, whom Jake recognized to be Casper from R&D, had on the same cloak as him, and also wielded a similar wooden bow. Casper was one of the few other people Jake always got along with during work. They had to interact a lot due to what they did and naturally hit it off. Both were rather introverted and happened to possess

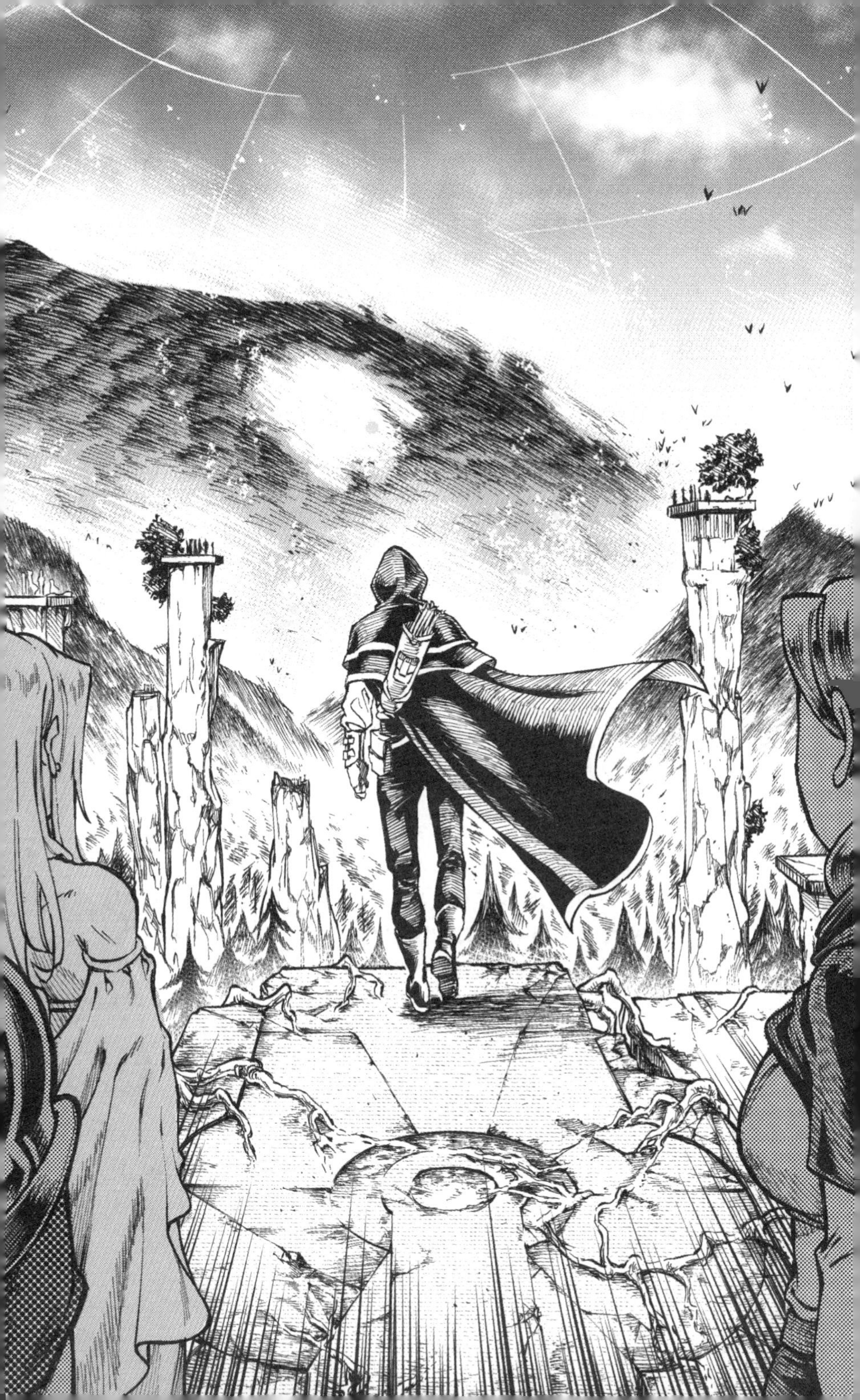

some of the same hobbies. He wasn't sure if he could classify him as a friend, but close acquaintance at least. Also, they both sucked at anything romantic, making them kindred spirits in that department.

Joanna was one of the people panicking the most, with her husband Mike not being amongst them. She herself had chosen to be a caster, perhaps just due to it seemingly being the least physically demanding. Though, thinking of it, she'd once said that she and her kids really liked a certain book about a scarred boy wizard.

He also learned from the conversation that he apparently could have asked for a different weapon in the introduction. Maybe he could have gotten a modern compound bow... though he doubted it, considering the whole medieval theme going on.

The last two classes were two other casters, all wearing brown robes very similar to the one he had on. These seemed to be quite a bit more comfortable, their material more akin to silk. They all had wooden sticks in their hands, something he assumed to be wands. And finally, there was their one healer, Caroline, in her white, silk-like robe with her smaller white wand.

Another topic discussed was naturally the skills granted. As Jake expected, everyone had gotten Identify and the translation skill included in the title granted upon entering this so-called tutorial. Class skills were another story, though.

Light warriors had a dual-wielding skill, which gave a boost while wielding two weapons, a throwing weapon skill, and a common-rarity skill, the counterpart to Jake's Archer's Eye called Quickstep, allowing the warrior to make quick bursts of speed. In reality, however, the skill just made one take a step slightly quicker than normal, being thoroughly underwhelming in practice.

The medium warrior had five skills, though all with Inferior rating. They had a skill for one-handed, one for two-handed, one for sword and shield, a throwing weapon skill, and an ability called Balanced Approach, which gave a small bonus to all stat effects while wielding any weapon. It was one so small that neither of the two medium warriors could even tell the difference.

The heavy warrior had the same sword-and-shield skill, a two-handed weapon skill, and a skill called Toughen Up, which allowed the warrior to make the effect of Toughness increase temporarily. That, too, was incredibly underwhelming, not even having any visual cue at all. Also, Bertram said it still hurt when Jacob jabbed him, making even the effect questionable.

The Archer skills Jake already knew, of course.

Casters also had three skills: a magic-tool proficiency, which allowed them to use their wands and other magic items, an attack skill called Mana Bolt, and a defensive skill called Mana Barrier. The barrier sucked too, being so weak that a casual swipe with a sword could break it, but the Mana Bolt seemed quite powerful.

The healer class also had three skills: Heal, which, unsurprisingly enough, allowed the healer to heal things, one called Regeneration, which turned out to be a passive aura that allowed allies of the healer to regenerate health faster, and the same magic-tool proficiency as the casters. Of these skills, Jake was especially interested in the aura, and how exactly it determined who were allies and who weren't.

Another thing they also determined was that the identification skill didn't work on other people. It did not even return a basic message. There simply was no response. It seemed that either the rarity of the skill was too low or prohibited for some reason. Jake looked toward Caroline and decided to ask about the aura, but he was interrupted before he had any chance to.

"Everyone, look at the other platforms," the heavy warrior, Bertram, said, grabbing everyone's attention. "I think there are other people on them."

As Jake looked over at the nearest platform, his improved vision came in handy, as he was able to make out some details. There appeared to be ten individuals on the other platform too, and as he looked around, he realized there were more populated platforms. He still saw some bursts of light on some of the other platforms, but after a minute or two, it was all silent, and the tutorial started for real.

Tutorial commencing
[Tutorial Panel]

Duration: 63 days & 21:47:11

Tutorial Type: Survival

Completion Criteria: Survive the duration of the tutorial.

Tutorial rules: Collect Tutorial Points (TP).

Tutorial Information: The Great Forest below is filled with danger and opportunities for the new initiates to experience. Beasts roam the forest, hunting for prey. Kill the beasts to acquire TP while gaining strength. Perhaps even a chance to hunt the Beast Lords will present itself...

Tutorial Point Rules: Gain TP upon killing beasts split amongst the contributors. Upon killing another initiate, half their TP will be split amongst the contributors.

Final Rewards based on TP and the number of Survivors.

Total Survivors Remaining: 1200/1200

TP Collected: 0

As Jake read through the information, he felt the pillar under him shake slightly, as it slowly began lowering. He quickly collected himself and checked that all his equipment was properly in place. As he did this, he wondered how he could be so calm despite the situation, then noticed that everyone else was also oddly calm, even if it did vary from person to person. Perhaps it had something to do with Willpower, or more likely, it was due to reliance on a certain individual.

Throughout the conversation, Jacob had been the guiding light for everything. He had made sure one person spoke at a time, that useful information was extracted, and that everyone got their turn. It was an unspoken rule that he was the leader of the group. One that Jake, of course, had absolutely no intention of opposing.

The group calmly discussed their plan of action during their descent, Jacob instantly taking the lead once more, of course.

They agreed to focus on the first aspect of this entire thing: survive. They all had weapons, and all had potions; warriors and archers had three health and stamina potions each, while the casters and Caroline had three health and mana potions instead.

Besides that, all they had were the clothes on their bodies. The rest of the internal discussion mainly revolved around the tutorial's weird details, such as the seemingly random duration. They also reached an agreement that hunting down beasts was a necessity. None of them was a fan of it, but they had to eat somehow. Based on the tutorial rules, it didn't appear possible to shy away from violence. They also collectively agreed that they wouldn't antagonize any other survivors unless they didn't have any other options.

Jake didn't agree with everything, but didn't want to play devil's advocate or start any unnecessary fights. He had already noticed from before that maybe he was a bit of an outlier. He didn't really understand the unwillingness to hunt. He himself felt quite excited at the notion.

"First of all, we will have to locate water, food, and shelter," Jacob said. "The flora does not appear to be the same as that on Earth, so we can't trust our current knowledge of what is and isn't safe to eat. We should try to see if the Identify skill can help with distinguishing edible from poisonous plants. The system also mentioned beasts, so hunting will likely also be an option, if not necessary, to secure a source of food. But we also have to be wary of the other survivors. We shouldn't be aggressive, but let's not be taken as pushovers either. Chances are we will have to hunt beasts as the system says to get stronger and survive. If we work together and do our best, I am sure we can all make it home safe."

The small speech was a bit superfluous, considering they had already gone over those points, but it seemed to get everyone on the same track. Jake was once again reminded of why Jacob was the youngest department chief their company had ever had. He had achieved this, relying solely on his competency and charisma, plus a bit of nepotism, but that was almost expected in the job market in this day and age, or, well, before this day and age.

The only thing that put Jake slightly off was spotting Caroline staring at Jacob with stars in her eyes. Not that

this was either the time or place for such silly thoughts. The pillar was getting closer and closer to the ground.

As they finally reached below the crown of the trees, Jake was able to spot several bird-like creatures hiding in the trees, though he was unable to make out any details. Two months... He would have to survive two months in this forest.

When they were only a few meters from the ground, Jake steeled himself for whatever was to come.

The pillar finally reached the ground, and they found themselves in a clearing. The pillar below them oddly seemed to phase through the ground, only leaving grass beneath their feet, and no evidence of the massive pillar ever having existed.

Taking a deep breath of the fresh air, Jake clenched his fist around his bow. He felt a bit nervous. But more than that, a weird feeling began bubbling up from deep inside of him. Excitement.

His boring world had changed, and he had no intention of making this damn forest his grave.

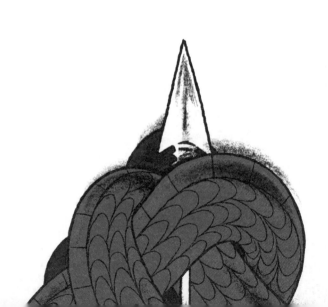

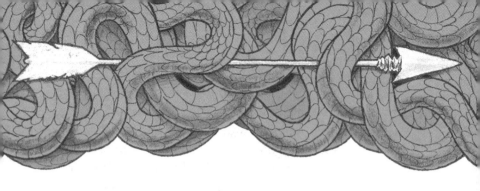

CHAPTER 4
FIRST BATTLE

The group had previously considered their immediate plan of action upon reaching the ground, with the first objective being to find somewhere safe to set up a camp. The artificial sun in the sky seemed to have moved a bit during their short stay, indicating a day-night cycle.

Bertram had made the educated guess that nighttime would prove even more dangerous than daytime. If beasts filled this forest, they guessed some of them had to be nocturnal. One couldn't ignore the threat of other humans taking advantage of the cover of darkness either.

After walking out of the clearing where the pillar had sunk into the ground, they wandered into the forest. The tension of everyone increased as they found themselves in a far more confined space. The first objective was to hopefully find a source of water to place their camp close to. Due to the trees' dense crowns, it was impossible to spot anything from up on the pillar, so they had to go in blind.

As they walked, gawking at the environment, Jake was weirdly relaxed. Despite his vigilance of whatever might lurk behind the trees around him, he had a feeling that nothing would sneak up on them. He still listened for potential dangers, of course—a difficult task, as it wasn't exactly the silent kind of forest. Birds sang, distant roars of beasts rang out frequently, and the rustling of the leaves as the wind swept through was louder than what he was used to. This was likely linked to his slightly higher Perception.

As their frontline heavy warrior, Bertram, went over a small hill, he suddenly came to a stop. Jacob quickly walked up to stand beside him. Jake was all the way in the back, but he could still hear them due to their proximity.

"What are those things?" Bertram asked as he looked down the hill at another small clearing. Jake walked up beside them, being the last to arrive. He looked down at a group of what he assumed to be the mentioned beasts of some sort.

"They look like large badgers," Jacob answered, turning to the rest of the group. "Though judging from the deer-like thing they are eating, I think they have upped their diet quite a bit. We already agreed that we might need to hunt. These things don't look very dangerous, so we should be able to handle them. Any thoughts?"

Jake looked at the big badgers. Four of them, each the size of German shepherds. Judging by how they ate the deer-thing, ripping the flesh away, they without a doubt had sharp teeth and claws. The perception of their surroundings seemed lackluster, though, to say the least. None of the things had noticed him or the others in his group yet, despite them only being thirty or so meters away.

The feeling they gave him wasn't one of danger at all. In fact, he had a feeling that handling them would be easy.

Interrupting Jake's thoughts, the other archer, Casper, pitched in, "I vote for hunting. From the roars in the distance, it sounds like much more dangerous things are around, and they may even be our source of dinner tonight. They seem to be low-level beasts."

That got a nod from Jacob. Hearing the word *level*, Jake mentally slapped himself in the face yet another time today, wondering why he hadn't tried to use Identify yet. *This is what the damn skill is for,* he thought grumpily.

Focusing on the beasts one by one, as he phased out the conversation around him and got what he'd hoped for—somewhat.

[??? – lvl 3]
[??? – lvl 4]
[??? – lvl 3]
[??? – lvl 3]

«... I'm just saying, maybe they are closer to ferrets than badgers!"

"I'm not saying they are not slightly ferret-like; I'm saying that you're confusing ferrets and weasels!"

Jake finally zoned back into the conversation, hearing Dennis, the light warrior of their little group, and Lina, one of the casters, arguing about something pointless. Not exactly surprising. They were cousins and had an ongoing, never-ending charade of pointless discussions going on, some spanning days or even weeks before they finally decided to "agree to disagree."

Jake had to confess he couldn't see the resemblance to either creature... but then again, he didn't know the difference between the two anyway. But he was pretty sure of one thing. Ferret or weasel, an arrow to the heart or head was lethal.

Breaking up the inane argument between the two cousins, the other medium warrior, Theodore, seemed to have had the same idea as Jake. "Guys, I just tried to use Identify on one of them, and it was level 3. I couldn't see the name, though."

"Oh, great initiative! Why didn't I think of that!" Jacob cheered and patted Theodore on his back. Turning to Jake, he asked, "Hey, Jake, do you have any thoughts on what to do?"

"No, but I also tried identifying them. Three of them are level 3, and one of them is 4." Jake had never done well in big groups like this, especially when all nine of the others turned his way. Seriously, he just hoped for the useless chatter to stop and the fighting to begin.

They were ten versus four. They had the jump. Every advantage was theirs, so this posturing felt... pointless.

"Okay, then, it seems like fighting them is the decision. Now for our tactical approach...»

Several more minutes passed laying down a strategy and deciding on how exactly to engage the beasts. After the earlier discussion, they had retreated behind the hill again to avoid the things spotting them. Peeking up over the hill occasionally, the badger-maybe-weasel-maybe-ferret-like beasts did not seem to be in any kind of a hurry with their meal.

The plan was simple: Fire off ranged attacks from a distance, trying to damage or maybe kill one or two, with Bertram trying to go in the front with his shield and get their attention, while Jacob and Theodore flanked him to cover his sides. The plan held the assumption that the beasts were stupid and aggressive if attacked.

Planning so much was maybe a bit overboard for overgrown badgers, but no one seemed willing to take any risk. A sentiment that Jake understood, but disagreed with. Wouldn't a fight without any risk be a bit... boring?

The only problem with the plan was that apparently the casters only had around ten meters of range on their bolts—any longer than that and they would fizzle out of existence, according to what Ahmed, the last of the casters in their group, had been told during the introduction.

They easily dismissed Dennis with his throwing daggers, having no faith in his accuracy at thirty meters, or even ten for that matter, assuming he could even throw them that far. This left Jake and Casper. And as for Casper... The first time he had ever held a bow in his life was earlier that same day when he got it from choosing the Archer class.

"So, Jake, you got confidence to hit one from here?" Jacob inquired, seemingly not holding much faith in the plan they had spent the last ten or so minutes making. That the planning had been a waste, Jake agreed on. The beasts would already be dead if it was up to him.

"Of course," Jake answered, once again slightly less awkward than before with everyone staring at him. His well-hidden frustration at the passive group outweighed his social anxiety.

He took out an arrow from the quiver on his back and inspected it. Wooden shaft, steel tip, and fletchings made of a kind of feather he did not immediately recognize. The weight was good and balanced, the arrowhead sharp, and overall, it seemed to be of good quality.

"Okay, ready when you are," Jacob said, getting ready along with everyone else. From the looks of everyone, the lack of confidence was all around. They weren't fighters. The only one who appeared to have some kind of proper training was Bertram.

Jake walked up over the small hill, followed by everyone else just behind him.

He looked at the beasts and nocked the arrow. He raised his bow as he focused. His vision instantly sharpened, instinctively knowing that Archer's Eye had activated. Time seemed to slow down ever so slightly as he pulled back the string.

For the first time today, something felt right. The morning routine, work, the introduction, and everything else was just... wrong. But at this one moment, as he held the bow, everything felt like it was as it should be. He smiled, took aim, and shot the arrow. Before even seeing the result, he had already taken out another arrow, preparing to shoot once again in one fluid motion.

The arrow had been aimed at the neck of the strongest beast, the one at level 4. He had briefly considered the heart or the head, but he had limited knowledge of their physiology. The heart might not have been placed where he assumed, and the hardness of the skull was way too unpredictable. The arrow flew in a straight line, with more speed, power, and accuracy than Jake had ever shot an arrow before.

The arrow hit the beast straight in the throat as it raised its head from the carcass of its prey.

It fell back over, and before the other badgers had even registered what had happened, the second arrow arrived, hitting the left-most badger square in its chest, penetrating deeply. The remaining two badgers looked over at the hill and instantly charged at Jake, showing no regard for their lives.

Before they had even moved five meters, another arrow arrived. This time, they were ready, however, and dodged a head-on hit, only leaving a shallow scratch on the one on the right as it dodged. Jake only managed to get off two more arrows before they arrived at the group, both leaving minor injuries on one of them.

Before the beasts could sink their teeth into Jake, a huge figure moved in front of him, carrying a huge shield and a shortsword, followed by Theodore and Jacob off to each of his sides. Jake flanked around, still hidden behind the three men in front of him, trying to see if he could get off another shot.

The first badger to reach them was the uninjured one, smashing into Bertram's shield and predictably getting knocked back from the impact. Following just behind it was the injured one, this one slightly more cautious as Jacob tried to keep it at a distance by pointing his sword at it and making threatening motions.

As Jake took his time to line up a shot, the beast that had smashed into the shield was stabbed by Theodore, who had somehow managed to get it in its hind legs. With the thing disabled, the two warriors quickly managed to hack away at it.

Jacob was still attempting to take on the injured badger, swinging his sword back and forth, with the beast jumping around and trying to attack him while not getting hit by the sword. Jacob had gotten several scratches on his arms already, and the badger also seemed to have taken a couple of hits.

Jake aimed his bow, and just as the badger jumped away from the swipe of the sword, Jake released the arrow, hitting the badger in the side. Before the thing had a chance to collect itself, Jacob's sword fell, cutting into its head and promptly ending its life.

Bertram and Theodore had also managed to finish off the last badger around the same time. Looking at the two initial ones he had hit, he saw both were also dead. The first one he had hit in the throat had died instantly, while the other one had managed to run a couple of meters toward them before it succumbed to its injury. Judging from the blood, Jake had hit something important, likely even the heart.

"Holy shit, we did it!" yelled Theodore, swinging his bloody sword around.

Behind them, Caroline was rushing up to Jacob. She started mumbling some words, and a white light appeared around her hands as cuts and bruises on Jacob's arms slowly healed. Jacob thanked her and looked over at Jake with a weird look in his eyes.

Jake did not feel like having any unnecessary social interaction, and as the adrenaline slowly wore off, he looked at the system messages he had missed during the fight.

You have slain [Badger Cub – lvl 4] – Bonus experience earned for killing an enemy above your level. 8 TP earned

'DING!' Class: [Archer] has reached level 1 – Stat points allocated, +1 Free Point

You have slain [Badger Cub – lvl 3] – Bonus experience earned for killing an enemy above your level. 4 TP earned

You have slain [Badger Cub – lvl 3] – Bonus experience earned for killing an enemy above your level. 2 TP earned

'DING!' Class: [Archer] has reached level 2 – Stat points allocated, +1 Free Point

'DING!' Race: [Human (G)] has reached level 1 – Stat points allocated, +1 Free Point

You have slain [Badger Cub – lvl 3] – Bonus experience earned killing an enemy above your level. 2 TP earned

Well, Jake thought, *that was a bit more than expected.* He felt good. Right. The warm glow from the increased stats sure helped, but it was more than that.

He had won. It had been an easy battle, but it still felt great. The feeling when he'd hit each of the badgers was still clear in his mind, carrying the satisfaction that came with every kill. He wanted to hunt more.

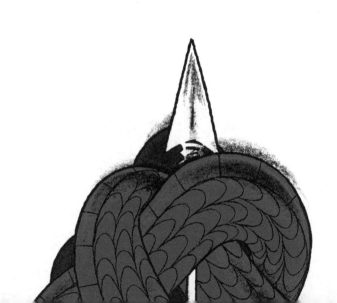

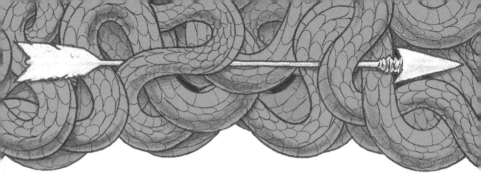

CHAPTER 5
BIG PIG

As Jake was still basking in the feeling of his level-ups and post-battle euphoria, he opened his status window. The reverie of his colleagues was of little interest to him, as while he enjoyed the victory, he didn't exactly view it as some monumental achievement. They were overgrown rodents... *Badgers are rodents, right?* Probably not. He moved on.

Status
Name: Jake Thayne
Race: [Human (G) – lvl 1]
Class: [Archer – lvl 2]
Profession: N/A
Health Points (HP): 130/130
Mana Points (MP): 120/120
Stamina: 111/130
Stats
Strength: 13
Agility: 14
Endurance: 13
Vitality: 13
Toughness: 11
Wisdom: 12

Intelligence: 12
Perception: 18
Willpower: 10
Free Points: 3

Titles
[Forerunner of the New World]

Thinking back, he hadn't opened the window since the introduction. Not even to confirm his class or title. And it sure had grown. His Agility alone had nearly doubled with the title and levels added together, going from 8 to 14. With Perception being the stat that increased by 2 points per Archer level, it had grown by an entire 8 points. And he could feel it. Sounds were clearer, and his vision sharper than ever—save for when he focused on using Archer's Eye.

It could be his imagination, but he felt like his Perception was still increasing as he stood there, venting down. Either the new stat points only applied their bonus gradually, or perhaps one simply needed time to get used to them. *Got to experiment with it*, he thought as he smiled to himself.

Stats were truly a weird thing. During the fight, he had moved faster and been stronger than ever before, at the level of an athlete in peak form, at least. Yet it had all felt so natural that he hadn't even questioned it for a second. It was almost scary how easy it was to adapt to his body's performance going through such huge changes.

Deciding to write it off as system-magic, he dismissed the status screen, finally noticing that everyone was either staring at him or the dead badgers.

"Thanks, Caroline," Jacob said as he gently pushed the now blushing Caroline away from him. He turned to the rest of them as he praised them. "Good job, everyone. Especially you, Jake."

Jacob seemed back to normal again, the same passive smile and glint in his eyes as before. The tension after the fight had left everyone by now. On a sidenote, Jake had entirely "ruined" their carefully made plan by killing half of the beasts before the fight even began, the only beneficial part of the plan still applicable being what to do with the corpses after. They needed a source of food, so... badger meat. Yay?

Figuring out how to transport the badgers was a hassle, as no one wanted to pick up the dead and bloody animals. Especially not the one killed by Bertram and Theodore, as it was a complete mess, filled with holes. They ended up only taking the two killed by Jake at the start of the fight, as they were the most whole. The carrying went to Ahmed, who felt bad for not contributing in the battle, and Dennis, who just seemed eager to help. No one even addressed or asked Jake to take anything. Not something he was going to complain about.

As they walked forward, still looking for any source of water, Jake checked his quiver and took note that he was down to fifty-four arrows, having fired six in the previous fight. Focusing on the quiver, he once again Identified it:

> [Enchanted Quiver (Common)] – A quiver enchanted with the ability to conjure common-rarity arrows when injected with mana.

Now I just have to figure out how to inject something with mana, he said to himself... only to figure out four seconds later that injecting something with mana was way easier than he had anticipated. He just had to hold it in his hands, and then think really hard about doing it. It was almost instinctual.

As the mana slowly left him, it felt a little weird, but not really uncomfortable. In the quiver, he saw arrows slowly appear, seemingly growing out of the sides of it. After half a minute or so, there were once again sixty arrows in the quiver. Trying to inject any more mana seemed to have no effect at all. Looking at his mana, he saw that he was down to 102/120.

So, three mana per arrow. Got it. Damn, this would have been useful back in the day. Admiring the magical quiver, he mentally added, Or not, as I didn't have mana...

He had considered recollecting the arrows, but there were several reasons not to. First of all, he would have to clean the arrows somehow before they were useful again. Secondly, their penetrative power would be reduced if already used once, if only by a little. Third... he could just magically conjure them. And if he started getting low on mana himself, he could just have one of the warriors fill it back up since they didn't use their mana for anything else.

All of that was ignoring how time-consuming it would be to recollect the arrows when it only took seconds to conjure new ones.

As they kept walking, Jake quickly ended up at the front, walking beside Bertram. Bertram seemed to hesitate about something, but eventually opened his mouth.

"Jake... were you in the military or something? Or maybe you went hunting from time to time?"

Jake was a bit taken aback, not expecting that kind of question. "No to both. But I did a lot of archery when I was younger, and still practice when I visit the old folks back home. Why are you asking?"

Jake was honestly confused. If he had to say so himself, he did decently in the last fight, but that was it.

"I just thought you handled yourself so well back there, nothing more," Bertram said, not pressing further, though he didn't seem like the answer satisfied him whatsoever.

Jake nodded at him and turned his head forward again, scanning the foliage. One thing he had noticed was the complete absence of insects or grubs or any of the smaller animals, really. There were birds up in the trees, but even they were all roughly the size of pigeons.

No insects were good, though. Normal animals seem to have mutated, or perhaps become something else entirely. Imagining mutated mosquitoes, ticks, or spiders, he could easily see their entire group being wiped out without even knowing how they died.

The forest was extremely dense and full of hills, fallen trees, and giant bushes, which made knowing what was ten meters ahead of him an uphill task. This made them move rather slowly, barely keeping up a walking pace.

After a couple more minutes of walking, Jake finally spotted some movement off to his left. He instantly poked Bertram in the side, who followed his line of sight, also seeing the rustling bush. Bertram lifted his arm, motioning the rest of the group to stop. Jake took the bow off his shoulder and took an arrow out of the quiver, nocking the arrow. He was ready for whatever was in there.

After a few moments, the bush stopped rustling, and everything went silent once more. As the seconds passed, everyone seemed to start relaxing. Everyone but Jake. His intuition told him there was still something in there.

He focused and used Archer's Eye, observing the bush very closely. He spotted light being reflected between the leaves, and without any hesitation, he loosed an arrow.

A huge shriek was heard, and stumbling out came a small boar, no taller than up to their knees. After stumbling for a few steps, it fell on the ground, an arrow sticking out of its left eye.

> *You have slain [Boar-Beast – lvl 1] –
> Experience earned. 1 TP earned*

Everything was once again silent as they stared at the dead pig. Jacob opened his mouth to say something, but was interrupted by an even louder sound.

A deafening squeal rang out, followed by the sound of stomping, causing the ground to vibrate slightly.

«RUN!»

Jake had no idea who had yelled, and he didn't need to think twice before following the advice. He ran back and found his way around one of the larger trees. Without hesitation, he took out his knife and another arrow from his quiver and slammed them into the tree, penetrating easily.

He started climbing as he registered the rest of his group, all running to hide behind the trees. Bertram was the only one still out in the open holding the rear. His shield was aimed toward the direction of the stomping.

Just as Jake was making rapid progress climbing up the tree, the bush where the small boar had come from earlier was torn apart. A massive boar, taller than even Bertram—the tallest member of their group—emerged.

The boar completely ignored Bertram and the others and charged straight at the tree Jake was climbing. It smashed tusk-first into the tree, making it shake excessively. The impact made him lose his grip on the arrow, but he managed to hang on to the knife and avoid falling to what would most likely be certain death.

As Jake stabilized himself by taking out another arrow and plunging it into the bark, the rest of the group stood frozen gathered around another tree nearby, everyone just gawking at the huge beast. Finally, Jacob got his shit together and called for the casters and Casper to start shooting spells and arrows at the thing.

The beast, completely ignoring the group of nine preparing to engage, instead kept smashing its head into the tree while making loud squeals. A bad move by it in retrospect, as it allowed enough time for the humans to attack.

Three bolts of mana, followed by a lone arrow shot into the boar's side, finally made it take proper notice of the other humans. The mana bolts made small explosions as they smashed into it, leaving small holes and burning its hide, while the arrow seemed unable to even penetrate the hide.

The massive boar, now with new, far more reachable targets, started stomping toward the group. No one, not even Bertram, had any intention of having a head-on test of strength with the thing, as they all started running behind the trees.

This had the effect of making it unable to charge toward them, as it tried in vain to impale anyone. They kept dodging behind trees, making use of the beast's inability to make tight turns and maneuver properly, buying time for Jake to climb up to a branch and secure a foothold.

From his new vantage point, Jake started shooting arrows at it. Compared to the arrows fired by Casper, Jake's penetrated its thick hide and embedded themselves in the beast. Once more, it tried to charge him, but it only ended up smashing into the tree harmlessly again in its stupidity, doing more damage to itself than anyone else.

What followed was what seemed like ages of Jake shooting the boar, the casters firing mana bolts whenever possible. Meanwhile, the warriors tried to keep the beast's attention on them by making loud noises and waving their hands and swords at it.

It all seemed to be working rather well until they all heard a yelp. Jake saw that Joanna had fallen over something and was now lying prone on the ground, within mere meters of the boar. She appeared completely out of it from the fall and didn't even look like she was trying to get up.

The boar was stupid without a doubt, but it was at least smart enough to recognize vulnerable prey when it saw it, as it instantly shifted its attention to her. Bertram tried running to help her without hesitation, but he was too far away and too slow as the beast charged Joanna.

It didn't even try to skewer her on its tusks—it simply charged over her. As its massive hooves smashed down across her, a loud snap was heard, followed by Joanna screaming in pain.

Before it could turn around and attack her again, Bertram finally reached it and stabbed his sword into its side, penetrating with nearly a third of his sword. The blow made it instantly change its focus to him and ignore the screaming woman.

With a fast swipe of its head, it smashed its tusks into the heavy warrior, sending him flying back and into a tree with a loud thud yet leaving the sword stuck in its side. However, this entire sequence of events did allow Dennis to reach Joanna and start dragging her behind a tree.

From Jake's vantage point, as he continued bombarding the beast with arrows, he saw everything. *Nothing to do about it*, he thought as he kept up the assault. He figured he should at least make use of the space created by the woman's ineptitude.

The beast was starting to look like a porcupine with all the arrows sticking out of it, and with the occasional mana bolt burning its flesh, the beast had started getting visibly slower in its movements. It huffed loudly, now staring red-eyed at Dennis, who was covered in Joanna's blood.

Before the beast could start another reckless charge, it was hit in the eye by another arrow fired by Jake. Attempting to grab another, Jake noticed his quiver was empty, as the beast charged the tree he was in once more. The blood was visibly pooling in the undergrowth, and the boar itself looked like it had been dipped in a bath of red paint. Another two mana bolts hit the boar in its hindquarters, and Casper was still firing arrows, though only dealing minor damage.

The beast was on its last legs by now, and the warriors finally felt confident enough to go closer. All of them started stabbing it, save for Bertram, who had been knocked into the tree pretty hard earlier. He was still conscious but struggling to get back up.

With a few more stabs, the warrior's swords—and the continuous blood loss—made the beast finally fall.

> *You have slain [Irontusk Boar – lvl 10] –
> Bonus experience earned for killing an enemy
> above your level. Experience split with the rest
> of your party. 302 TP earned*
>
> *'DING!' Class: [Archer] has reached level 3 –
> Stat points allocated, +1 Free Point*

Jake felt the warm glow of the level but decided that bothering with the notifications could wait. Jake jumped down from the tree and rushed to where Joanna was lying. Caroline was already with her, using her healing magic. As he got closer, he was initially relieved that she was still alive, until he saw her lower body. One of the legs was completely ruined, while the other was missing entirely from the knee down. The massive weight of the boar had smashed it entirely into paste.

"Use the healing potions too!" Ahmed yelled, taking out one of his and handing it to Dennis, who supported her head.

Dennis quickly uncorked the bottle and poured the red liquid into Joanna's mouth.

The effect was immediate as the smashed leg started rapidly healing, and Theodore quickly grabbed it and put it in a proper position, ignoring the screams from the former receptionist. The leg healed, but the situation on the dismembered one was less positive. While the wound did close, no new limb was regrown.

Bertram slowly walked over, holding an empty bottle in his hand. Judging from his condition, he must have also consumed a healing potion. Joanna had lost consciousness, likely due to the pain, and the mood had turned even more somber than before. There was no post-victory celebration this time.

"We need to move," Ahmed said with a sigh. "This much blood is bound to attract something."

Dennis and Theodore decided to carry Joanna with one supporting each shoulder. The two badger corpses had both been dropped when the boar rushed at them, and quite frankly, no one felt like looking for them. Besides, there was a chance they'd been trampled to pieces by the Jeep-sized beast.

As they started walking, Jake took his quiver in his hand and began conjuring more arrows in case another fight broke out. They couldn't let a minor setback like this stop their hunt. There was still daylight left.

Just as four arrows had been generated, Jacob and Caroline both slowed down and ended up walking beside him.

Jake was still wondering what they wanted when Jacob turned to him and looked him in the eyes.

«...Why did you do that?"

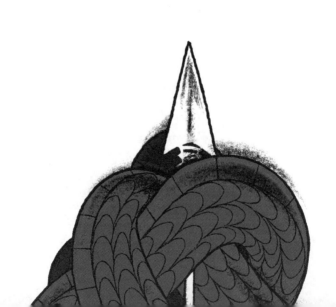

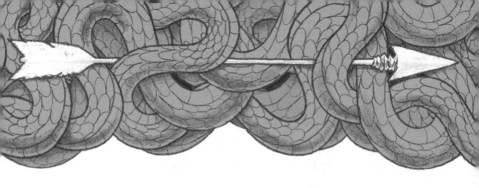

Chapter 6
Questioning

Jake was taken aback as he looked at Jacob with confusion clear on his face. "Why did I do what?"

With a lowered voice, making sure no one else could hear them, Jacob elaborated. "Why did you decide to provoke the boars without any thought, not consulting anyone in the group? Look what happened. Joanna lost her damn leg, Jake. We are in a god-forsaken forest filled with monsters that want to eat us, and within mere hours, one of us is crippled.

"What do you suggest we do now? Bunker down and hope nothing finds us for over two whole months? Or, what, leave Joanna behind to die? What exactly was your plan when you decided to shoot into a bush, without having any goddamn clue what was in there? There are other people in this forest too—what if it had been one of them? What the fuck is wrong with you?"

Jacob's face got visibly redder as he kept barraging Jake. He also grew louder and, of course, got the attention of the others. Everyone was staring at them by now, and, looking around, Jake spotted open hostility in some of their eyes, with others looking down at the ground. Bertram and

Casper both just looked sad, while Ahmed didn't have any emotions visible on his face. However, he didn't seem inclined to voice his opinions.

Jake had never seen Jacob this angry before. *Right, what was I thinking?* He'd just seen a reflection of something. In hindsight, it was the eye of the small boar. Something in his head had told him to shoot. It was just... instinct.

Indeed, he hadn't been thinking. From the beginning, he hadn't. Except for his internal pondering, when it came to any kind of combat or tense situation for that matter, he gladly ran on autopilot. He allowed his instincts to take over and intuition to be his guiding light when making split-second decisions.

"I... I am sorry, I was just... I don't know..." Jake couldn't properly express himself, his incompetence at social situations once again evident. On the one hand, he did feel bad about the outcome of the situation, but he didn't truly think it was his fault.

Not taking the shot would have been stupid too. It could have been a predator waiting to ambush them or even a trap of some kind. Besides, it was a foe they could clearly handle. The only reason why Joanna had ended up like she had was that she'd screwed up and tripped.

"You don't know?" Jacob said. "Well, you should know! Just think, for god's sake! We are humans, not beasts who attack anything we see. Think about the consequences. We are a group. A team. What would have happened if we hadn't been here? What if you had been alone?" Jacob got more and more aggrieved with Jake's passive demeanor and lack of feedback to his critique. Not due to Jake not taking it to heart, but because he simply had no idea how to respond.

He took the question very much to heart. What would have happened if he had been alone? Replaying the fight, he began from the beginning.

He'd been climbing the tree when the boar came out of the bushes and ran toward him, already out of reach of the beast. While it did make him temporarily lose his grip, he was never really in any danger of falling. The increased stats made him stronger, faster, and he had no problem holding himself up with only one arm. With his stats, he would have thus been able to climb the tree quite easily.

The arrows he'd fired into the beast had done more than enough damage to make it bleed to death eventually. Toward the end, more than fifty arrows had penetrated it, and even if he had run out, he could've started conjuring more. Ultimately, the boar would've been forced to leave or stay below the tree and wait for him to keep shooting. And judging by the behavior of the thing, it likely would have stayed until it succumbed.

The tree was more than strong enough to take the hits, having barely taken any damage. With its circumference easily being large enough for seven or eight grown men to stand holding hands around it, he saw no scenario where it would be falling over. So, to sum it all up... if he had been alone, he would have gotten solo experience and TP, and no one would have gotten seriously hurt, though the fight would have taken longer.

On top of that, Jake had an inherent unwillingness to ignore his own instincts and intuition. As most people would, he assumed. While he in his work-life before the system was very calculating, always taking an analytical and data-based approach, he also relied on his guts a lot. The same for tests in university. He trusted his intuition to an almost unhealthy degree.

When it came to archery, and pretty much everything else in life, he had grown to prefer taking everything as it came, trusting in his own judgment.

And he felt like his instincts and intuition had only gotten stronger after the system came. Even taking a more objective look at his performance in this tutorial so far, he had made little to no mistakes... If he was alone, that is.

He had made correct split-decision choices. With every arrow he shot, he'd never second-guessed if he should shoot or not. What if he had hesitated to climb the tree for even a second? He would likely have been squashed to mush in between a tree and a giant pig.

Judging by the behavior of every beast they had encountered so far, the small boar had been likely to attack them either way, making the fight with the big boar inevitable. The result of his actions may not have been optimal, but he still adamantly stood behind them. Killing the small boar had been the right decision, and his performance during the fight was as good as anyone could expect.

"I did what I deemed best, and I do stand behind the decision to kill the small boar. Even if it had been another human, trusting anyone not from our team is a horrible idea. The tutorial actively encourages us to kill each other. Don't forget that." As he spoke, he found confidence he hadn't quite known he had.

"Jacob, this new reality of ours is one where magic exists. Joanna is hurt, but she isn't in danger. She lost a leg, but who is to say that cannot be healed? With her improved physique, she should be fine soon, and maybe we can even attempt to make a wooden leg or something for her. Or we can just have her guard our camp since she can cast magic. This isn't our old world anymore. People die. I would count us lucky to not have lost anyone yet. Seriously, look at the tutorial panel, everyone."

The final part of his sentence, spoken loudly, addressed everyone. Jake himself had opened his panel already:

[Tutorial Panel]
Duration: 63 days & 20:52:39
Total Survivors Remaining: 1112/1200
TP Collected: 319

Not even an hour had passed since the beginning, and yet nearly a hundred people had died. And Jake seriously doubted that beasts were the only culprits behind the many deaths.

The others were silent, unsure of what to say. It was no secret that Jake had been the main contributor of the group so far, performing the best in combat and scouting ahead for potential dangers. He'd even led them away once from an area where Jake felt like strong beasts were fighting each other.

Despite them having been here for so little time, and only being in two fights, Jake had more than shown his proficiency. Even Jacob, the de-facto leader of their group, had to admit that Jake had been the one doing most of the heavy lifting so far.

"Jake... I just want you to remember that we are a team. Consult with us, tell us your thoughts before just jumping into motion. To not be making the decision for all of us..." Jacob sighed, not willing to dwell on the topic anymore. He seemed relieved that Jake had no intent to either. "Let's keep moving forward."

The following half an hour was uneventful, Jake still walking at the front with Bertram just a bit behind him, and the rest of the group silently following his lead. Finally, as it was also starting to get slightly darker, Jake heard the subtle sound of running water off in the distance.

He once again thanked his improved senses and told the group what he heard. Everyone was relieved, and after only another five minutes, they made their way to the top of a hill and saw a small river running just downhill. It was minimal, barely a couple of meters wide, with depth only to one's ankles, but a source of fresh water was a source of fresh water.

The group quickly found a clearing just a bit down-stream and settled down on the grass. For the first time since the beginning of this tutorial, everyone finally re-laxed—except Jake, who was sitting with his quiver in hand.

Jake had conjured more arrows on the way but started getting a headache. A symptom of low mana, it seemed, as his mana had dropped down to 11/120. Stamina was still looking fine at 116/140. The maximum had been in-creased by 10 due to the point in Endurance given by the level-up in his class. Looking at his stats, he was once again reminded of his 4 unallocated Free Points.

The biggest challenge in the prior fight had been his ability to deal damage. Against small targets, his arrows dealt major damage, and he could aim for vital spots. Like the boar, large creatures were simply too big to get affected much by the small arrows.

There were weak spots, like when he hit the eye, but the other weak spots were normally protected. It had tak-en him his entire quiver of arrows to down one big piggie, and that was with help. But he wasn't sure if a couple of stat points in Strength or Agility would in any way en-able him to do any serious damage. There was simply too much fur, skin, flesh, and muscle to get through before he hit any organs.

Saving the points seemed like a waste too. After think-ing a while, he decided to put 1 point in Strength, 1 in Agil-ity, and 2 in Perception, just following his class distribu-tion. Looking at his stats, not much had changed, except the points from a single level-up and the Free Points.

Stats
Strength: 15
Agility: 16
Endurance: 14
Vitality: 13
Toughness: 11
Wisdom: 12
Intelligence: 12
Perception: 22
Willpower: 10
Free Points: 0

Looking around, he was clearly not the only one consulting his menu screens. The chatter started shortly after; everyone just happy to finally have a modicum of safety. No one spoke to Jake, which was fine, as he was happy just to listen in.

Everyone had gotten a single level in their race and class from the kill on the boar, it seemed, Bertram even gaining two in his class. He had already gotten one level in his class from the first fight with the badgers, but his contribution against the boar seemed to net him quite a lot.

After having relaxed for twenty minutes or so, the peace was broken by Jacob getting up, urging the group to not waste what daylight was left. Distributing tasks, they began gathering firewood, checking the perimeter, and getting materials to perhaps make some basic tools. Theodore had the idea of taking some of the vines lying around and perhaps making some makeshift rope. The vines were very thin, but rather strong, and could be woven together.

Surveying the perimeter went to Jake, who ended up killing two more badgers who were lurking in the bushes just outside the clearing. They were only level 2, giving no levels and only 4 TP. Since Jake didn't have enough mana to recharge all his arrows, Casper gave him some of his arrows to fill up his quiver. Afterward, he started spending his own mana to conjure more, effectively acting as a mobile arrow factory.

This also allowed him to ask Jake for tips related to archery and combat in general. While even Jake was surprised by his own level of competence in combat, he was more than confident and willing to give advice on how to handle a bow. He had tried to go pro when he was younger, though he didn't exactly go around bragging about it, mainly due to the fact that he had to give up that dream because of an injury, leaving a bit of a mental scar.

He demonstrated proper forms and advised on aiming, proper motions when taking arrows from the quiver, nocking them properly, drawing the bow, and finally releasing the arrow, all in one fluid movement. Casper stood at his side, trying to follow along with the movements while throwing in a question here and there.

Around the two archers, everyone was busy trying to make at least a barebones functional camp, and Ahmed volunteered to try to skin and prepare the two badgers Jake had killed that skulked at the outskirts of the clearing. His goal was to make it possible to cook them.

Jake and Casper were left alone to their own antics, spending hours of training with their bows. As Jake thought back on all his knowledge of how to use a bow through teaching Casper, he was pleasantly surprised by the system suddenly giving him a notification.

Skill Upgraded: [Basic Archery (Inferior)] – An Archer's best friend is the bow in his hand and the arrow in his foe's heart. Unlocks basic proficiency with bows and crossbows, and adds a minuscule bonus to the effect of Agility and Strength when using a ranged weapon.

-->

[Advanced Archery (Common)] – An Archer's best friend is the bow in his hand and the arrow in his foe's heart. You have shown improved proficiency with a bow, making the weapon even more familiar to you. Adds a minor bonus to the effect of Agility and Strength when using a ranged weapon.

The stats' bonus effect went from minuscule to minor, though Jake still had no clue exactly how big the effect was. His bow did not really feel any more familiar than before, perhaps because he already felt very comfortable with it.

Casper, while not getting any skill upgrade, still showed quite an improvement in his abilities. While it was certainly getting darker, there was still quite a bit of sunlight left in the day, and the dinner preparations were far from ready.

Jake still had a few things he wanted to test. Looking at Casper while thinking of what to do, Jake got a brilliant idea.

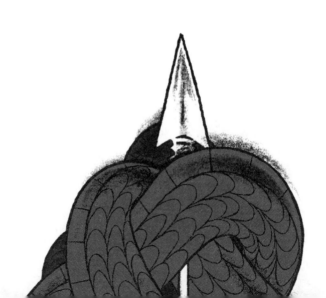

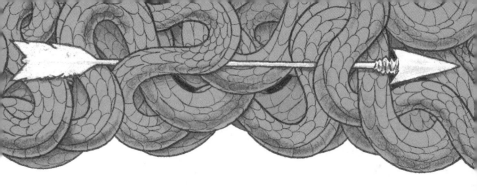

Chapter 7
Training & Rest

"OW! For fuck's sake, that hurts!" Jake growled after being hit by yet another arrow.

"Jake, are you sure about this?" Casper asked, genuinely wondering if Jake was actually a masochist. He had been shooting padded arrows—which used dulled arrowheads wrapped in cloth—at Jake for nearly three hours already. The cloth had come from Jake's own jacket, which he had been wearing under his cloak this entire time.

"Yeah, just give me a second," Jake said, getting ready once again. He had wrapped the torn sleeve of his jacket around his eyes, acting as a blindfold.

"Are you *really* sure this is doing anything? Well, I guess it's good target practice for me, but..." Casper mumbled the last part.

Jake's plan was rather straightforward. He would have Casper shoot arrows at him while blindfolded, then try to react to them without relying on sight.

While Jake certainly had reservations about his own plan's veracity to begin with, he had made progress throughout their training session. In the beginning, he'd merely flinched milliseconds before the arrows hit. Now he could at least try to evade the arrow before it hit him.

"Just keep the arrows coming; I can feel it!" Jake said, still hurting yet very positive.

He had been wondering about his weird senses since coming to this tutorial. He'd somehow "known" the big boar was charging through the bushes before he saw or even heard the beast. Actually, to say he *knew* was a bit too strong of a word. He'd just had this vague feeling that a massive danger was coming.

In combat, he didn't really think much, per se, but merely went with the flow. He was still in full control of his body, of course, but at times, it felt like his brain couldn't keep up with his body. His instincts. He just did what felt most natural at the time. And the results spoke for themselves.

And that was how Jake got the idea for this kind of practice. He wanted to train his senses and allow him to understand exactly what was happening to him and why it felt like he had a new sixth sense. He had suspected it had something to do with being an Archer or with the Perception stat, but Casper didn't have the same experiences as him at all.

At the beginning of their impromptu practice session, Casper had merely thrown small sticks and cloth-wrapped stones at him. Jake had felt nearly nothing before the things hit him. He could get a feeling that something was coming toward him, but not how fast or where it would hit. It had also come way too late for him to react.

After quite a bit of frustration and thinking, he'd asked if Casper could throw a rock not wrapped in cloth. This time, he'd felt it quite vividly before it hit him, and even more so when it actually did hit. Got a nice blue mark from that one. A round of Casper apologizing profusely later,

Jake had calmed him down and convinced him to switch to the cloth-wrapped arrows. They still hurt like hell, but at least they were not able to cause any real damage. Well, he had lost a few health points, but it was barely notice-able, and they were regenerating quite quickly.

Throughout the session, Jake felt the improvement more and more, and he felt like he was just a little away from grasping something. He had a far more distinct feel-ing that something was about to hit him than when he started. Still not enough of a feeling to react adequately, though.

Back in the present, the next arrow came, and Jake once again felt that something was about to hit him, so he tried dodging it. He ended up still getting hit again and even ended up tripping while trying to dodge it. He got up again, not at all discouraged. He had felt it there. Not just the concept of danger approaching, he had even felt *what* it was that was about to strike him.

They kept up the practice a bit more, with Jake even managing to dodge an arrow or two here and there. Casper was finally beginning to believe in whatever Jake was do-ing, and even asking questions about how to do it. Jake tried to explain the feeling he got, but he sucked at putting the feeling into words. Besides, it was like trying to explain colors to a blind person.

Another hour went by before someone came over from the makeshift camp. Food had been prepared, and while neither Jake nor Casper were hungry, they knew the importance of sustenance. No one knew when they would get their next meal either.

The dinner that was about to be ready was the two badgers killed earlier, grilled haphazardly over a small fire after being skinned and gutted. Bertram knew how to do that, surprisingly. They didn't have any spices or proper tools, though, so frankly, it looked quite... simple.

Even the cook, Lina, had to admit that it did not exactly look appetizing in any way. Caroline was the one that came over to the two archers to get them to eat. Jake nearly felt like all the pain had been worth it when she sat down next to him in order to heal his wounds as he ate. The healing felt good, like a cold stream running through his veins, and he saw the blue marks slowly disappear over the next twenty minutes as he sat there, enjoying the sensation.

They chatted while Caroline mainly asked questions about why he had let Casper use him for target practice for the better part of four hours, and about other minor things, like how he was so good at using a bow and whatnot.

Jake was happy to talk to her, and explained his training with Casper and what he hoped to achieve by doing it. He also explained to her how he had practiced archery growing up and how he still did it from time to time.

He even divulged how he'd sadly had to give up going pro due to an injury, much to Caroline's interest. She had always seen him as the silent, nerdy type, and not at all sporty. This also made Jake realize how little he had interacted with her outside of work. The same went for everyone in their group, in fact.

He had never been the social type in any kind of setting, really. While he wasn't absolutely hopeless in social interactions, he did try to minimize them.

Him liking Jacob and Caroline was most likely because they were two of the only people outside of his family that he felt comfortable around. Because of his welcoming nature and open demeanor, Jacob allowed pretty much anyone to feel good about themselves. Caroline, on the other hand... He couldn't put his finger on why he liked her. He just did. Ah, who was he kidding? He just found her physically attractive, and that was about it. He'd barely known the gal before the system.

In university, he had purposefully worked on improving his social skills and actively aimed to take part in gatherings and such. While he never got completely comfortable doing it, it improved his self-confidence tremendously during those years. Getting a girlfriend and a few close friends did even more for that confidence to develop. All until it was brought down the day he walked in on his girlfriend and his supposed best friend. Apparently, it had been an open secret in their little group. Open to everyone but Jake.

All the work and development he had gone through had been for naught, and his self-confidence and self-worth were tossed in the gutter. His girlfriend had claimed it was just "having fun" and that it was nothing serious, while his so-called best friend had seemed to think it was no big deal at all, and that he just had to "stop being a pussy about it." This was a sentiment apparently shared by everyone else in their little university group. Or maybe they'd just feared social excommunication from the group if they spoke up.

This event had led to Jake returning to his old, introverted ways. He'd studied, done archery, played games, watched TV, and gone to classes. A good day was one where he hadn't spoken a single word to anyone but his parents when they called, asking how he was doing.

It had improved after he graduated, having gotten a good job, one through which he was forced to engage in the social system that is the workplace. Jacob was the one that had gotten him out of his shell initially and made him open up more to his colleagues. Enough to be on friendly terms with everyone, at least. Jacob seemed to always try to invite Jake to things explicitly. Thinking back, the reason why they were in this tutorial together was maybe even due to Jacob asking him to go to lunch together.

In a professional setting, he had no issue speaking or expressing himself normally now. The same reason why he had no problem arguing for his decision-making with Jacob earlier and talking with Casper during their training. But what he was doing right now? Casually small talking with Caroline... It was more nerve-wracking than facing down the huge boar.

During the conversation, Dennis yelled out to them, clearly flustered.

"Caroline! Joanna woke up. Can you come check on her?" All of this was said while nervously shooting glances at Jake. Caroline did not hesitate and excused herself as she followed Dennis over to Joanna. Not that they were very far away, being less than five meters from where they had been sitting and eating.

Jake could easily peek or listen in but decided against it. He wouldn't blame Joanna if she were angry at him. In her eyes, he was the indirect cause of her injury, after all. However, he was a bit scared she would put any of those thoughts into words or actions.

How would he react if she started yelling at him? Blaming him? Could he stand there and argue that he stood by his decision? Or would it get heated and turn into another huge argument? He was afraid to find out, and fell back into his old habit of simply avoiding the potential confrontation.

He closed his eyes and once again focused on trying to understand and reexperience his weird new sixth-sense-like ability. As he closed himself off mentally, he lost track of time until he was awoken by Casper, who was about to poke him in the side.

Jake opened his eyes before the finger even touched him, much to Casper's surprise. Jake was about to ask what he wanted when he noticed Jacob having gotten up also. Clearly about to launch into another speech.

"Alright, everyone, we made it through our first day," he said as he gave a sad look Joanna's way. "Casper already checked and confirmed that the beasts have at least some fear of fire; however, we are not sure if it is a sure thing. I think we should have someone be on watch while everyone sleeps. We should make a rotation."

No one had any objections to the idea of having someone watch their back as they slept. It was agreed that two people would keep watch together, while the others slept. Making the rotation, they had an odd number of potential lookouts, Joanna being excluded from the rotation. Without much fuss, Jake volunteered to keep watch solo, once again not meeting any objections.

The first watch would be Lina and Dennis, the second watch would go to Jake, and the third to Jacob and Caroline. Jake wasn't exactly overjoyed imagining Caroline and Jacob being alone together, sitting at a bonfire under the moonlight. Not that a murder-forest was particularly romantic.

As they finished cleaning up after dinner, nobody wasted any time getting some shuteye. While the stamina of most of them was still more than half full, they were nevertheless exhausted. While Jake did not feel particularly tired, he knew it would be foolish not to take the opportunity to get some sleep in. It wasn't exactly comfortable, just lying on the grass—the coarse cloak offered little comfort.

Jake shut his eyes and fell asleep immediately. Quite a feat, considering the circumstances. He had no idea exactly how long he had been sleeping—he imagined the three hours they had agreed on—but he woke up as he felt someone approach him. Opening his eyes, instantly alert, he heard Lina give a small yelp as she jumped back, frightened by Jake's sudden awakening.

"Holy shit, you scared me," Lina whispered. "Were you already awake?"

Jake got up and made sure he had his bow, full quiver, and knife still on him. "No, I just woke up. How long have I been sleeping? And did anything happen while I slept?"

He looked around. It was now deep in the night, though not as dark as he would have assumed. The moonlight did much to illuminate the surroundings, making it quite easy to see everything in the clearing. Or perhaps it was just his improved eyesight making everything appear brighter. He frankly had no way to know.

"We have been keeping watch for a bit over three hours," she said. "We used the tutorial countdown to keep track, and nothing has happened, really. A couple of small animals and what looked like more of those badgers were on the outskirts of the clearing, but they didn't even exit the bushes or get close to us. Scared of the fire, I think. That, or my awesome magic!"

Jake chuckled at her attempt at a joke, mainly out of courtesy. He could see how tense she was and knew she was just trying to lighten the mood. She smiled, and they went over to Dennis, who was more than happy to be relieved of his services.

The two promptly went over to the others to sleep, while wishing Jake a peaceful watch. Jake took a seat on the same log that Dennis had been sitting on as he looked into the dark forest. *Let's hope that the rest of the night will also be quiet.*

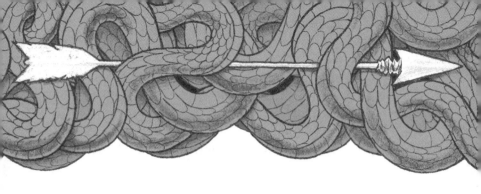

Chapter 8
A Wonderful Night

The night was quiet, far quieter than one would expect from a forest filled with borderline mindless beasts who wanted nothing more than to munch on human flesh. There were no roars, no howls of wolves or hoots of owls. No sounds at all, really, except the breeze rustling the trees and bushes, and the crackling of the bonfire.

The responsibility of the person on watch was quite simple: keep an eye out for things trying to kill them, and keep the bonfire lit. Jake checked his stamina, seeing it up to 135/140. Nearly maxed out again by around three hours of sleep. It had only been at around half when he went to sleep, regenerating far faster than he had predicted.

The need for sleep being reduced with levels was certainly a possibility, or perhaps the introduction to the system had changed something fundamental that simply made sleep less important. For example, Jake was wondering what would happen if one just chugged down stamina potions whenever it got low. Perhaps one could stay awake indefinitely.

Shaking his head, Jake got up and took a short walk around the camp, surveying the perimeter of the small clearing. In hindsight, the location of their camp was poorly chosen, to say the least. There were trees and dense bushes all around them, making easy hiding spots for any predators, and not a single direction offered any solid cover from potential assaults.

Jake considered if they should look for a cave or something like that in the morning. Then again, caves also had their drawbacks, as chances were there would only be one entrance… and he could just imagine a beast like the big boar charging through the narrow tunnels, trampling anything in its wake. Yeah, not a pretty picture.

Looking at the trees, it seemed possible to somehow make camp up in one of the larger ones, though that would make having a fire impossible, and he was not completely confident in everybody's ability to climb said trees.

Thinking about how little activity there was in the forest at this time of night made Jake think that the system—or whatever or whoever had designed this tutorial—was not completely ruthless. The absence of nocturnal beasts made surviving quite a bit easier, giving them time to sleep and recuperate. Even animals like badgers, which were normally active at night, seemed to only hunt during the daytime.

Jake, however, still had to remain vigilant, as he had no solid evidence that there were no beasts out there still hunting. He could also not forget the other humans of the tutorial. He had seen them on the giant pillar at the start, spread out to all sides. Thinking back on it, he realized they had only been to the left and right, and none in front or behind him. He also couldn't forget the giant wall off to the back of them.

The space between the pillars was measured in kilometers easily, so it was not surprising that they had not run into other survivors yet. It had only been half a day or so, and while they had been moving for a while, they had not gone far, perhaps only a few kilometers tops. The pace had been slow, everyone moving tensely and overly carefully, even taking some detours to avoid potentially dangerous areas. The direction they had traveled was also directly away from the wall.

He didn't even know if all the other participants in the tutorial were actually human. He had seen silhouettes, indicating bipedal creatures, but he had no way to know if they just had roughly the same shape as humans, or if they *were* humans. And quite honestly, he was not sure if he preferred for them to be humans or for them to be aliens, as chances were they would end up in conflict at some point.

As the minutes slowly ticked by, the monotony started getting to him. While sitting still and just keeping an eye out may sound easy, anyone who has worked any kind of night job knows exactly how boring it is. But sadly, reading a book or playing on his phone was not an option.

Dennis and Lina had likely kept themselves entertained by talking and keeping the other awake and aware. The boredom, mixed with the lack of even the slightest stimulation from the environment, led to Jake slowly becoming less and less vigilant.

However, he was promptly awoken from his stupor once more when he heard rustling from one of the bushes at the far end of the clearing, the furthest away from the bonfire. Jake fixed his eyes on it as the bush kept rustling. He did not feel any sense of danger from the bush as he focused on it, but his instinct nevertheless told him something was wrong. That he should be careful.

He took his bow and got up from the log, checking back on everyone still soundly asleep. Everyone had been dead tired yesterday, mainly due to the mental exhaustion of this whole ordeal, so he was not at all inclined to wake them up for a false alarm.

He walked toward the bush, which still rustled slightly once every couple of seconds as he got closer. He scanned the bush, seeing nothing but still feeling hesitant to go right up to it. He started drawing his bow and aimed it at the bush, then slowly walked closer, taking tiny steps and preparing for anything that might jump out.

Without any warning, something came out of the bush, and he instantly shot his arrow, easily hitting it. At the same time, before he could even register what it was, a silhouette charged out from the bushes. He couldn't properly see what it was in the darkness, but the humanoid silhouette was clear. It was further cemented when he saw the moonlight reflected off the blade of a sword.

Jake stumbled backward and called out to awaken the others, but the sound had barely left his mouth when he haphazardly raised his bow to try and block the sword.

He managed to block it, but he was pushed backward, once more nearly falling to the ground. He barely held on to the bow with both hands. Finally, he got a proper look at the assailant. It was a bearded man who seemed to be in his thirties, wearing an outfit identical to the one worn by Jacob and Theodore. In other words, a medium warrior.

The warrior once more tried to swing his blade, but it had cut into the wood of Jake's bow and gotten stuck. Their fight became a stalemate—Jake trying to get his bow back and retreat, and the warrior trying to cut all the way through and into Jake's body. However, the stalemate was short-lived as another person rushed out of a nearby bush, wielding a huge two-handed axe.

Jake saw him, and it didn't take a genius to know the situation was bad. Real bad. The medium warrior was as strong, if not slightly stronger, than Jake, and he had already been forced into close combat, meaning he had no way to use his bow. The others back at the camp had awoken by now, but they were scrambling and confused, with not even one of them having a clue what was going on. Jake and his attackers were a good twenty-five meters from the bonfire, hidden in the darkness.

Jake was at a loss what to do as the axe-wielding warrior got closer. He had no time to think, so instead of thinking... he just reacted. Less than a second before the axe smashed his head in, he let go of his bow just as the warrior tugged, making him fall backward from his own momentum. Jake took the opportunity to pull back as the axe smashed into the ground where he had just stood. The weapon was now stuck in the ground, making the heavy warrior his next target.

Charging forward, he tried stabbing the heavy warrior with his knife but was blocked by the man's armored arm. Without any hesitation, Jake pulled an arrow from his quiver and, making use of the arrow's length, managed to hit the axe wielder's eye with an overhead blow, just reaching across his guard. The arrow barely penetrated, but it was enough to buy him time.

When he turned around, the medium warrior was once again upon him, but Jake managed to block the first strike with his knife. The warrior took a step back and swung his sword once more, but this time, there was a slight red gleam around it; it moved faster and was far stronger. Jake's attempt to block it was met with severe pain in his wrist as the knife flew out of his hand.

At the very same time, he felt a distinct sense of danger from behind him. No... not the feeling of danger, but that of sure death. Time seemed to get slower, as Jake's senses were stimulated like never before. He saw—no, *felt*—the battlefield. The axe wielder had gotten up once more, bleeding from his eye, but had managed to pick up his axe and prepare to attack again.

The medium warrior was already upon him once more, raising his sword for another strike. Even more importantly was that behind him... an arrow was flying for his head. For the first time ever, he completely embraced the feeling of these new, unfamiliar senses. But even more than that, he completely and unquestioningly followed exactly what his instinct told him to do. Something had been unlocked, and he more than willingly accepted it.

He swayed slightly to the side, raising his left hand behind his back as he caught the arrow. The same motion easily dodged the overhead blow from the medium warrior as he slammed the arrow into the man's hand, making him yell out in pain and drop the sword. The axe-wielding warrior behind him once more tried to strike him, but he dodged the blow by ducking beneath it as if he had eyes behind his back. In the same motion, he caught the falling sword that the medium warrior had dropped earlier.

In a swift, fluid motion, he smashed the sword into the axe warrior's kneecap, making him buckle over as he screamed. Instead of trying to finish him off, Jake went for the medium warrior with the intent to finish off the now disarmed man. Jake ran toward him and cut him once across his arms as he raised them to try and block. The second blow sliced his neck open, spraying blood and drenching Jake from head to toe.

Another arrow flew his way, but Jake merely swayed slightly to dodge it as he rushed the axe-wielding heavy warrior, who was trying to pick up his axe once more. Jake, however, did not give him time to do so. In a full sprint, he kicked the man in the head. Before the disoriented warrior could recollect himself, Jake lifted the sword and stabbed it downward into the skull of the kneeling man. With his

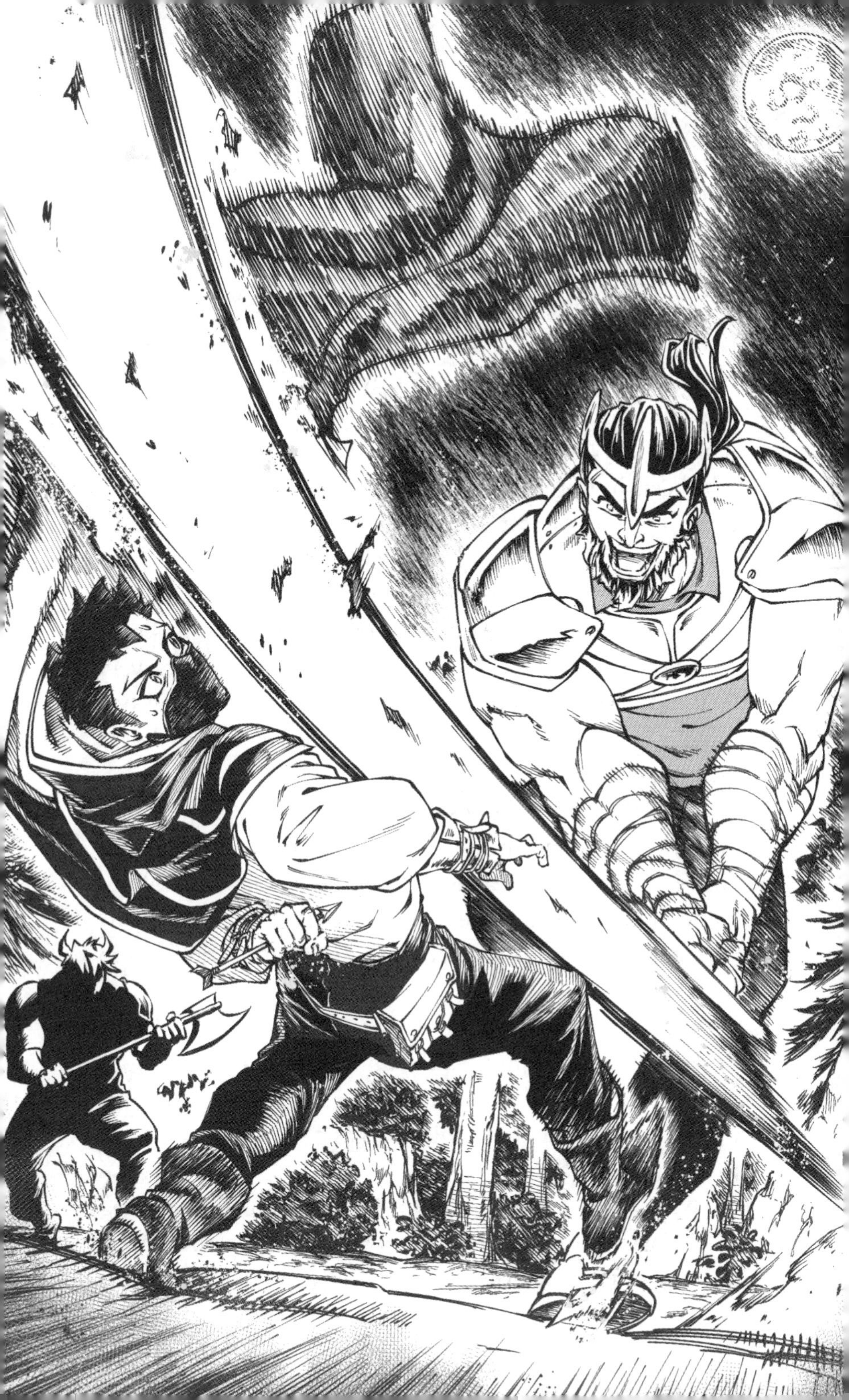

entire weight behind the blow, the sword still ended up only penetrating a few centimeters, but it was more than enough to pierce deep into the brain, killing the man instantly.

However, the sword was stuck, making Jake take out two arrows from his quiver and wield one in each hand as he dodged another arrow shot by the enemy archer. The attacking archer was clearly flustered, and fear was evident in his eyes as the blood-covered Jake charged him. He had been hiding in some bushes off to the side, but pinpointing him using the trajectory of the arrow was simplicity itself.

The archer threw his bow to the ground, realizing that he had no time to fire another arrow, and drew his knife. An excellent choice, as Jake had found his archery very lacking. Clearly a novice before the system, and he had a feeling the man wasn't that much better with a melee weapon either.

Jake smirked as he easily dodged the first swipe of the knife, then leaned in and stabbed an arrow into the archer's knife-wielding arm. To the man's credit, he did not let go of his knife, but it helped him little as another arrow was stabbed into his stomach. He dropped his knife from the shock of that one.

He tried fighting back, but Jake easily took out another arrow from his quiver and smashed it into the archer's chest, followed by another, and then another. The poor man was only able to flail his arms as he attempted in vain to ward them off.

Nine arrows later, the man finally stopped struggling as his last breath left him. A total of twelve arrows were sticking out of his corpse.

Jake got up and looked toward the sky, a small smile still on his lips. The sense of danger had passed, and his instinct to kill had gone quiet. He had survived.

The others back in the camp were now more than awake and ran toward him, all of them clearly still flustered. The moment they saw the scene, they were instantly horrified by the sight. A man lying facedown in a pool of blood, right beside another man still in a kneeling position, blood dripping from his eye and a sword sticking out of the top of his skull. The picture was made all the more horrifying by a smiling Jake, completely covered in blood, standing over another corpse with a dozen arrows sticking out of it.

"What... what happened?" Jacob stammered, clearly disturbed by the carnage.

A smiling Jake turned to him, still savoring the euphoric feeling he was currently experiencing. His smile grew even larger as he answered.

"I won."

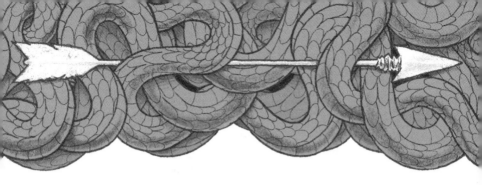

CHAPTER 9
BLOOD

Jake felt good. Incredibly good, in fact. The sensations that came from facing down certain death and coming out on top were wonderful. He didn't notice the weird look Jacob was giving him, nor did he notice that the other people in his group had made their way over, though some of them quickly turned right back around when they saw the scene.

Among the new arrivals, Caroline looked at Jake with a mix of concern and fear.

"Are you hurt? There is so much blood..." she said in a quiet voice. She looked pale as she stared at the image of Jake standing beside a man full of arrows, the blood gleaming as it reflected the moonlight.

"I'm good. None of it is mine." Jake said this casually, with a light smile. He was hoping to finish up any potential conversations so he could move on to more important things. He had gotten several system notifications that he was more than eager to get to.

"Oh... okay," she answered tentatively.

Caroline didn't seem inclined to ask any more questions, while Jacob looked like he had something to say, but chose not to.

Jake gladly took the opportunity to extricate himself when no one else spoke up. "I'm gonna go sit down and check my status messages. There are no more enemies as far as I can tell, so relax, everyone." He considered if he should tell them they could go back to sleep. He decided not to, as he had serious doubts anyone felt like sleeping right now. He sure as hell didn't; his spirits were way too high.

Jake walked to the bonfire, which was still burning bright as ever, sat down on the same log he had used as a lookout earlier in the night, and finally opened his notifications window to a slew of messages.

> *You have slain [Human (G) - lvl 3 / Warrior (Medium) - lvl 7] – Bonus experience earned for killing an enemy above your level. 478 TP earned*
>
> *You have slain [Human (G) - lvl 2 / Warrior (Heavy) - lvl 5] – Bonus experience earned for killing an enemy above your level. 340 TP earned*
>
> *You have slain [Human (G) - lvl 2 / Archer - lvl 4] – Bonus experience earned for killing an enemy above your level. 294 TP earned*
>
> *'DING!' Class: [Archer] has reached level 4 – Stat points allocated, +1 Free Point*
>
> *'DING!' Race: [Human (G)] has reached level 2 - Stat points allocated, +1 Free Point*
>
> *'DING!' Class: [Archer] has reached level 5 – Stat points allocated, +1 Free Point*

He had won not because of his stats, but purely due to how he fought. They were amateurs, and Jake doubted they'd even used all their skills during the fight. Besides the medium warrior using that glowing sword, he hadn't noticed anything else... Then again, they were all low level, and it wasn't like skills actually had any real visual prompt from what he had seen so far. In fact, he wondered if he should be surprised that the guy had a skill to make his sword glow like that to begin with.

Looking at his gains from the fight, the stat points and levels were nice, but the real gains came in the next few notifications, though they were a bit different from any earlier ones.

> *Bloodline Detected*
> Processing...
> ...
> Bloodline analyzed.
> *Bloodline Awakened*: [Bloodline of the Primal Hunter (Bloodline Ability - Unique)]
> – Dormant power lies in the very essence of your being. A unique, innate ability awakened in the Bloodline of the newly initiated human, Jake Thayne. Enhances innate instincts. Enhances the ability to perceive your surroundings. Enhances Perception of danger. +5% to Perception.

A new skill had been unlocked—or was it an ability? He was clueless as to what the whole Bloodline business was about. His family background was nothing extraordinary, as average as one could be, and yet he apparently possessed an innate ability tied to it.

Not that he was going to complain just because he was a bit confused. The effects of the ability were, in

Jake's honest opinion, awesome. It also explained why he had these weird senses that none of the others seemed to have. More amazing was that the description even included his name. That was kind of cool in its own right... right?

What he gathered from his own experiences, along with the description of the ability, was that it had four effects. The first one was the enhancement of instincts. Without a doubt, this was the explanation behind his performance in combat and the occasionally supernatural reaction time he possessed. His ability to react was way beyond what his stats should allow him, and the reason why he, at times, felt like his body couldn't keep up with what he wanted it to do.

The second part of the ability was the one to perceive his surroundings. The three-hundred-sixty-degree perception he had experienced during the fight made him act as if he had eyes in his back. He could not explain at all how it worked; he just "knew" where everything was.

Even now, it was still active. He "felt" the bonfire's flickering flames and every particle of smoke that entered the air. He "knew" of the log beneath him, how it had a small part of it inside that was hollow, and every single blade of grass around it. His understanding improved whenever he focused on it, but it was passively making him aware of roughly everything around himself, especially any movements.

It was all vague, however, and the range seemed only to be a few meters. He could not sense the others, as they were still at the corpses ten or so meters away. He estimated the range to be perhaps five or six meters. Too low for scouting, but invaluable in combat.

Third on the list was the perception of danger. That part was rather self-explanatory, honestly. It was the prickling sensation he felt whenever something dangerous was heading his way, the feeling in his gut that something dangerous was lurking ahead.

That part alone was great, but what made this part of the ability incredibly strong was the synergy with the two other effects. His perception of the area around him allowed him to perceive the nature of the danger, and his enhanced instincts allowed him to make a split-second reaction.

The fourth and final part was a 5% stat bonus to Perception. While certainly valuable, he saw it as rather inconsequential compared to the other effects. He didn't doubt it would prove more beneficial as he got more stat points, and the bonus started adding up, though.

The entire skill seemed far stronger than anything else. Archer's Eye was also a Perception-based skill, but compared to his Bloodline of the Primal Hunter, it was borderline useless for anything other than scouting.

Even with the ability itself being so awesome, it didn't come alone, bringing even more benefits.

Title Earned: [Bloodline Patriarch] – Unlock a unique Bloodline ability. The power found in the origin of your Records are yours, and yours alone to wield and pass down throughout the multiverse. May your Bloodline prevail. +15 Vitality, +10% to Vitality.

This one was... massive, in a few different ways.

The description of the title was quite something in itself, especially compared to his only other title, which was just a matter-of-fact statement that he was now part of the multiverse and new to it. This one instead talked about something called Records. Whatever the hell that was.

Even the name of the title felt quite a bit more impactful. Bloodline Patriarch. It was indicating that he was the forefather of the Bloodline and that it was his alone. Did this mean that the rest of his family didn't also possess it? Was he just the first one to unlock it? The thought of his family still alive briefly entered his mind, but he suppressed the thought. Now wasn't the time to get sentimental.

The description and stat points granted by the title indicated the system's desire for him to survive and thereby allow the Bloodline to live on... and oh boy, the stats. A massive +15 Vitality, instantly making it his highest stat, only made better by another +10% straight on top.

Looking at his stats, he found they had gone through quite a development from the level-ups, ability, and title.

Status
Name: Jake Thayne
Race: [Human (G) – lvl 2]
Class: [Archer – lvl 5]
Profession: N/A
Health Points (HP): 302/310
Mana Points (MP): 123/130
Stamina: 144/170
Stats
Strength: 18
Agility: 19
Endurance: 17
Vitality: 31
Toughness: 12
Wisdom: 13
Intelligence: 13
Perception: 28
Willpower: 11
Free Points: 3

His stats had seen a massive growth, which made him smile widely. He did frown a bit, however, as he began to question his Vitality being at 31. According to his quick math, he should have 29 Vitality before the +10%, having been at 13 the last time he checked. After that, he had gotten +1 point from his race leveling up and +15 from the title. With +10%, he should be at 31.9... and yet it only showed 31 and not 32. Did it only show whole numbers rounded down?

Jake had 3 Free Points, so instead of thinking further on it, he simply allocated a single point and saw it instantly jump from 31 to 33. *So, only whole numbers rounded down. Got it,* he thought, nodding internally.

As for his last two points, he decided to do another experiment. His stamina was at 144/170, being higher than his maximum was when he'd woken up earlier in the night. What Jake wanted to know was how increasing the maximum of a resource affected the current amount available.

He allocated a Free Point to Endurance, leaving him with one left for later. He saw his stamina jump to 154/180, adding a static 10 points to both maximum and current. *Does this mean you could potentially have infinite stamina with enough repeated level-ups?* Jake wondered, though he did admit the scenario of that happening was quite far-fetched.

For the last Free Point, he was unsure how to distribute it, so he just let it be for now. The last subject on his lengthy list of system messages was the result of reaching level 5 in his Archer class:

> ***Archer class skill available***

Jake mentally acknowledged that he wanted to browse class skills, and a big list appeared before him. To his surprise, a huge number of weapon skills showed up. *[Basic Two-Handed Weapons (Inferior)]*, *[Basic Shield Technique (Inferior)]*, *[Basic Unarmed (Inferior)]*, *[Basic Throwing Weapons (Inferior)]*, and so on and so forth.

The only ones he did not seem to have were the magic-related ones. Quite honestly, Jake was not interested in any of them whatsoever. He was more than happy with his already once upgraded *[Advanced Archery (Common)]*, and he still had the *[Basic One-Handed Weapons (Inferior)]*, in case things got dicey and he was forced into melee as he had been in the last fight. This left him with only three options available at the bottom.

[Basic Trapping (Inferior)] – The Archer is not limited to direct combat, but can also use his tactical prowess to emerge victorious. Unlocks proficiency using basic traps and knowledge of how to construct them. Adds a minuscule bonus to stat effects on traps based on the nature of said trap.

[Basic Stealth (Inferior)] – The deadliest predator is the one not seen coming. Unlocks basic proficiency in the art of stealth, allowing you to remain undetected more easily and blend into the environment. Adds a minuscule bonus to the effect of Agility and Perception when successfully remaining undetected.

[Basic Tracking (Inferior)] – The first objective of any hunt is to find your prey. Unlocks basic proficiency in tracking entities you

are familiar with. Must be identifiable tracks
available. Adds a minuscule bonus to the
effect of Perception when tracking.

All of them were just more basic proficiency skills.
Thinking back to the two melee ambushers earlier, both
had been over level 5 in their classes. He would not at all be
surprised if they both had the basic stealth skill, considering how close he'd gotten to them, while they'd managed
to remain hidden. Though the first warrior had a glowing
weapon, so he must have gotten a skill to do that. Yeah,
that made Jake a bit jealous. Good riddance; that lucky guy
was dead.

He saw value in all of them, but he did not see himself setting up a large number of traps, especially not with
his Bloodline ability. He very much wanted the tracking
skill, and he did consider taking it to track down where the
three attackers had come from.

But ultimately, he decided on **[Basic Stealth (Inferi-
or)]**. He could imagine the synergy with his Bloodline ability, allowing him to attack his foes before they would ever
get a chance to strike back. The fact that it also scaled with
both Agility and Perception only made it all the better.

The fight had made him realize how little he had ac-
complished since he got into the tutorial. They were all
higher level than him, with the medium warrior being level 7 in his class, more than twice what he had been. He had
already decided that he would need to go hunting.

He picked the skill and felt the same feeling as when
he'd gotten his class the first time. This time, it was far
weaker, though. It gave him something he wasn't quite
sure if he could call "knowledge," but he still instinctively
understood it. Maybe it was due to his Bloodline ability,

but he doubted it. Either way, he now knew how to sneak a bit better than before. It was a small, subtle thing, and far from a complete guide on becoming a master thief.

Closing all the menus, he felt very satisfied with himself, though perhaps a bit sad that getting a new skill was so anticlimactic. No ability to shoot laser beams or to shoot down the eight suns with eight arrows was gained.

Jake finally got up from the log and stretched his back. The smell of iron instantly reminded him that he was still covered in blood. Or, more accurately, his cloak and face were covered. He took off his cloak, seeing that his shirt and pants underneath were spared from the torrent of blood. Quickly, he sprinted down to the small river nearby, cleansed his face, and sprinted back up to the camp once more, the entire trip taking less than a minute.

As he felt refreshed, he also began to feel oddly naked. He immediately realized that he had no weapons on him whatsoever. His knife had been disarmed, and his bow had been hacked in two. He saw that the others were still over at the corpses, and Jake started walking over. He first got to the dead archer and picked up the bow he had dropped, noting that it was identical to his old one, the only difference being that this one was undamaged.

While picking up the bow, he couldn't help looking at the dead archer and the arrows still sticking out of him. The blood had long stopped seeping out, but the man's eyes were still wide open, showing visible horror. Jake looked at him as he stopped. He looked over at the other corpses: the man with a sword still stuck in his skull, and the other lying in a pool of his own blood.

At the same time, he saw the looks everyone gave him. It wasn't the same look of the blame for causing Joanna's injuries like before. It was one of fear. That was when it struck him, far later than it should have.

The attackers were humans. He had just murdered three human beings.

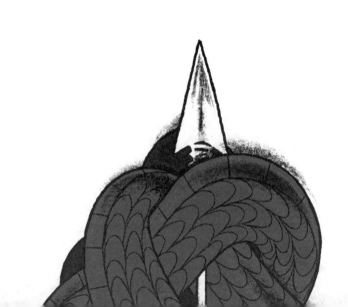

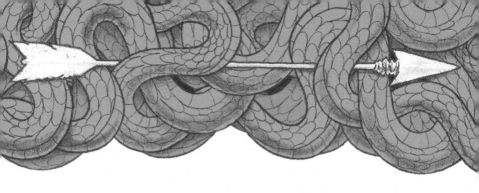

CHAPTER 10
REFLECTION & FRUSTRATION

Murder. Killing. Homicide.

The act of taking another human's life has many names in society. No matter the name assigned, it is a crime. It is immoral. And even if morals were completely ignored, the act of removing another member from society is, in most cases, a detriment to said society. The act of ending another life is innately abhorrent to humans, and even if the act is one hundred percent justified, it will often leave the killer traumatized by the experience.

In many comics, the moment a hero kills a villain, he becomes a villain himself. It is seen as a turning point for the character—his or her fall to the dark side.

These were just some of the thoughts bouncing around in Jake's head as he was sitting on the grass, staring down at the ground, reflecting on his feelings of what had transpired that night.

He had killed not just one, but three people. Logically, he knew that it was self-defense. They had tried to kill him, so he'd killed them instead. It was justified, and in many countries, could even be considered legal. Heck, it could even be argued that he was in a situation comparable to a war zone, making the laws of war apply, in which case he had simply killed enemy combatants.

Even if he got over the fact that he had killed them, though, the way he had done so couldn't be ignored. He had not thought of the ferocity of his actions during the fight, but as he saw the corpses, it couldn't be clearer how brutal he had been. Especially with the archer... He had pinned him down and simply kept stabbing him over and over with arrows until he finally stopped moving. It was a textbook example of excessive force.

The acts of brutality could perhaps be explained by Jake's inexperience in combat, the adrenaline pumping through him as he fought, and his enhanced instincts taking charge, but what he could not explain away was how he'd felt while doing it... and after. He'd felt nothing when he killed them. It was like he was just checking off three items on a list as he ended their lives one by one.

After the fighting, the only thing he'd felt was euphoria. He had never felt better. More alive. The relief, feeling of superiority, and overpowering sensation of "winning" were just too intense, too addicting. If the feeling was due to his enhanced instincts, as he suspected... that meant his base instinct, him at the very core of his being, enjoyed killing.

No, that's wrong, he corrected himself. He had not felt any pleasure from killing the badgers, and he hadn't felt any particularly strong emotions after the big boar either. He'd only felt contentment after that. He did not enjoy the simple act of killing... he enjoyed the hunt. The challenge of the kill. He enjoyed the feeling of winning over his foe.

Jake had never been the confrontational or aggressive type; in fact, he strived to avoid conflict whenever possible. But he enjoyed a challenge. He enjoyed pushing himself to his limits and trying to improve. Throwing his entire being into something and striving for the top. It was why he had managed to get so good at archery. It was how he had managed to graduate as one of the best in his class. Not because he was particularly smart; he just liked to see the number on his test score go up, so he slaved away to make it happen.

He remembered one of his professors describing him as "driven" and "ambitious." Jake wasn't sure if he agreed with either of those, but he did enjoy picking hard fights and coming out on top. What people misunderstood, though, was that it wasn't because of the reward from the challenge. He did it for the challenge itself. The outcome wasn't necessarily relevant.

That was how he felt about the fight that had ultimately resulted in the death of three human beings too. He felt like the outcome, their deaths, was ultimately irrelevant. It was the process of the fight that was his goal, and not the death of the three of them. It was just the unavoidable result of a life-and-death battle.

Which was the root of his problem. After reflecting on his emotions and boiling everything down, he came to the realization that he just didn't care much. Be they human or beast, in the end, they were just challenges to overcome. The only feeling of remorse or regret he'd felt so far in this tutorial was when Joanna got hurt.

Even then, Jake knew that he thought it was her own fault more so than his. A part of him hated feeling that, but when he thought the scenario over, he just couldn't find anyone else to blame but her.

She could not have tripped, to begin with. As a caster, she could have at least tried to use the Mana Barrier that they'd already established all casters had. Freezing up right after tripping sure hadn't helped her chances either. If she hadn't, rolling out of the way of the charge would have been more than possible.

If all those failed, she could at least have managed to avoid getting a limb trampled off so they could fix it up with a potion like the other leg. In other words, if it had been him in her position during the fight, he wouldn't have ended up losing a leg.

But it had happened, and she was now just a burden. He and everyone else in the group were aware of it, but no one truly wanted to voice it out. Leaving her behind was no different than leaving her to die. None of them wanted that on their conscience, and no one wanted to leave a colleague and a friend behind. Not even Jake, despite his annoyance at her. But at the same time, he couldn't stay like this forever.

He finally realized he did not fit in with the group, likely a bit late in retrospect. They were corporate workers, civilians in every sense of the word. The only fighting any of them had ever participated in was sports like boxing. He doubted any one of their entire group had ever even been in a barfight or something similar, except for one person.

Bertram did stand out. He'd been decisive and strong even before the tutorial. He handled his shield and sword well, and he didn't hesitate when attacking. The man had the eyes and demeanor of a fighter and was, without a doubt, the strongest person in the group except for Jake, but he was tethered to Jacob. Comparing their ragtag group of office workers to the ones he had killed was night and day.

While still amateurs with their weapons, the ambushers that attacked him had been far from new to fighting. They'd had a plan of attack, a damn good one in his opinion, and they'd had the guts to fight. They'd had the courage to take on the lookout of a group of ten with only three people. Their hope had likely been to kill him quickly before he'd even had time to wake up the others, then proceed to wipe out their entire camp before they could muster a counterattack.

Their levels also spoke to their proficiency. They had either dared to hunt down beasts or other humans to get their level, meaning they had fought most of the time since entering the tutorial. They'd just been unlucky to encounter Jake as the lookout. If it had been anyone else, chances were that the majority of their group would be dead now.

Comparing those three to his own party just felt sad. They would likely have lost several people to that big boar, if not been wiped out completely, if Jake had not been there. Maybe they would even have suffered injuries from the first group of badgers. They were weak—not just in fighting strength, but also resolve.

He realized that this line of thought was a spiraling black hole of negativity, but he had to acknowledge it. If his instinct, his natural disposition, was to enjoy hunting and overcoming challenges, then he could only see himself driven completely mad by suppressing those desires.

He finally looked up from the grass, having found a semblance of resolve. He would hunt, and he would grow stronger.

The others were still talking over at the two warriors' corpses, and Jake could hear their discussions, which seemed to mainly revolve around who the attackers were, where they'd come from, and if there were more of them. Jake looked at them. They were his friends, his colleagues, and, in the case of Caroline, his crush. He wanted them to live, from the bottom of his heart.

In order to make that happen, he needed power. He had won today, but would he win tomorrow? What if there had been more attackers? What if they had been higher level, or he had made a mistake? His Bloodline ability was far from flawless. It did not grant him omniscience, but merely faster and more appropriate reactions during combat.

Take the medium warrior's attack, where his blade had been coated in the red gleam. His instinct had no warning of it, and he'd ended up disarmed and nearly dead. The strike hadn't been a danger to him directly, as it hadn't been aimed at his body, only his knife. It had been an attack to disarm him, and his natural instincts couldn't recognize a complex attack like that. He also needed to think more while fighting and merge instinct and logic.

With his resolve steeled, he walked over to the rest of the group, save for Lina, who was still beside Joanna.

"Jake... can you tell us what happened?" Jacob asked as he saw him walking over.

Everyone seemed to avoid looking at the corpses, which was perfectly understandable. It was equally understandable that they avoided looking at the killer.

"Yeah... I was keeping watch when I heard...»

He explained exactly what had happened, and he saw the concern on Jacob's face as he described the ambush. The concern only seemed to grow into confusion as he described how he had turned the situation around.

"But... why would they attack us without reason?" Caroline asked.

"Experience, equipment, and tutorial points," Jake answered promptly. He then went on to explain the points he had gotten along with the levels. He purposely left out the whole Bloodline thing, though. The fact that one of the assailants had been level 7 came as a big shock to them, as the strongest of them, Bertram, was still only level 2 in his class after the boar kill.

"But to just murder someone…" Caroline mumbled as she instantly gave Jake a mixed look.

"It was self-defense, Caroline," Jacob said, coming to Jake's aid. «He… We have no choice but to defend ourselves. He may have saved us all. Please don't blame him for that. We may need to reconsider our strategy for…»

As the others kept talking, mainly filled with concern for the future, Jake went over and picked up the knife he had dropped when the medium warrior attacked him with the glowy-weapon skill. As he picked it up, he also finally solved the mystery of what had been thrown at him when they first jumped him.

He saw a dead badger, with the arrow he had shot stuck in it. It had been dead before he even hit it, with what looked like a long sword-cut across its stomach—something he presumed had been the cause of its death, to begin with. He doubted he would get tricked like that again with his new Sphere of Perception, the name he'd settled on for his new spherical vision.

Tuning back in to the ongoing conversation of his colleagues, he wasn't exactly pleased. The group discussion seemed to steer toward finding a safe place to hide and wait the tutorial out, only fighting when absolutely necessary or to get food. As Jake listened, he started getting more and more pissed off. Was he really the only one who had any grasp of the situation they were in?

He finally snapped as he started speaking in a voice far louder than any one of them was used to, using enough curse words that it would demand a call from HR.

"Wake the fuck up, people! This entire fucking tutorial is focused on killing! Oh, and it is called a bloody TUTORIAL! As in TRAINING! What do you people think it's a tutorial for? A nice corporate office job? Or, I don't know, maybe somewhere even more fucked up than this place?

What do you guys think is more probable? The world has changed, and you all need to get your asses moving and adapt if you want to survive."

Jake got winded toward the end, everyone just staring at him with wide eyes. He was perfectly aware that the outburst was entirely out of character. He'd just had enough. He had resolved that he wanted them to live, that he wanted them to make it through this tutorial in one piece, and they wanted to hide in a hole in the ground for over two months?

A single person who had fought just a little during the tutorial would be able to wipe them out easily in just a few days if they didn't gain any Strength. A random beast could come upon them and kill them too. Jake did not like to have the thought, but he was confident that the current him could take down all of them singlehandedly in an ambush, just picking them off one by one with arrows from a distance.

"What do you suggest we do?" Bertram asked as he stepped up. He had been the bravest and most competent by far in the group, not including Jake. He had walked in front, and he had even selected a class during the introduction that allowed him to defend others. The tone in his voice was not one of anger or confrontation, but sincerity.

"I suggest you do whatever you need to level up and survive this shit," Jake said. "Even if you don't want to fight other people, you at least need the strength to defend yourself when they wanna fight you. In other words, hunt beasts. Get experience, get power, do what the system wants you to."

"I agree with Jake," Casper said as he also joined the conversation. "We need to learn how to fend for ourselves. What if Jake had not been on watch, but someone else? What if they had come a couple of hours earlier? Would you be confident in fighting three people at once who were all above you in level, Dennis?"

Dennis shook his head, clear that he would likely be a corpse on the ground right now had the watch plan been different.

Jake hoped that his outburst could be a wake-up call for all of them. He didn't want to just leave them and go be on his own. He was afraid of the consequences of that. They couldn't survive on their own as they were now.

He gave them space to think it over as he excused himself from the group and went to check the corpses, starting with the two dead warriors. He knelt on the ground and started rummaging through their satchels. If he and his colleagues had gotten six potions at the tutorial's start, so had these people. He quickly took the satchels off the corpses and looked inside. Both had quite a number of potions in them, a mix of stamina, health, and mana.

The presence of the mana potions confirmed that these three had either been a part of a team with casters or healers who'd died, or they had killed casters or priests. He personally leaned toward the latter. There was a total of fourteen health, eight stamina, and five mana potions, also counting the contents of the dead archer's satchel.

He turned to the group once more, who had simply stared at him as he looted. It was still dark, but the fire from makeshift torches they had brought over made the scene well lit. The problem was that the forest was still too dark to leave. They would have to wait for morning before they could do anything.

"For now, try and get some more rest," Jake said. "It is still my turn to sit lookout, so I will. Get some energy. Tomorrow, we hunt." Then he sat down on his log once more, doubting any of them would get even a wink of sleep.

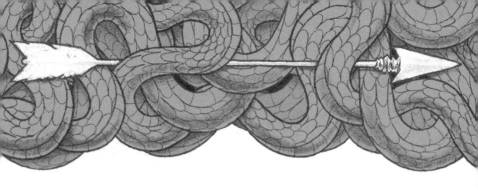

CHAPTER 11
FRIEND OR FOE?

J ake kept his promise of being on the lookout for the rest of the night. It turned out to only be a couple of uneventful hours until the artificial sun rose once more. Looking on as the scrambling group got up and gathered their things, he seriously doubted they had gotten any sleep at all.

Their current campsite was compromised, and they had no clue if more enemies would come, so they needed to find somewhere new. Their entire initial plan of finding water and food and all the usual survival crap turned out to be a damn waste of time. While they still needed food and water, they needed levels far more, so sitting in one spot was just stupid.

They got packed up, and Jake was surprised to see even Joanna up and about with a makeshift wooden leg. It was essentially just a big stick of wood bound to her thigh and what was left of her leg. It looked uncomfortable and certainly not fit for any big movements, but he saw determination and grit to keep going on her face. Jake felt respect for the woman, as she refused help, and they started walking.

They moved further away from the huge wall in the distance. Jake had a theory, based on where the pillars had been and the wall only being visible behind them, that this entire place had a spherical design. The fake celestial bodies also indicated a dome shape. Moving inwards toward the center of the dome would hopefully allow them to find more beasts. They had been very sparse in the outer area, after all.

It took little time before they came across another group of beasts. This time, it was a group of deer-like creatures, the very same that the badgers had been eating on the first day. There were seven of them total, and after using Identify, he found them to be between level 2 and 4, with the biggest among them at level 5.

Jake decided not to interfere, first of all because he was not sure how much experience killing lower-leveled enemies would give, and also because the entire purpose of this exercise was for everyone to build fighting experience. They started once more forming a long, elaborate plan, but Jake shut them down real hard and told them to get their shit together and move.

They had three casters and an archer, plenty of ranged firepower to take down some of them before the fight would even truly begin. Jake had given them all the potions he had looted the day before, so they were more than covered in that department. He did keep the stamina potions, though, as they were rather unnecessary for his colleagues at this point, and Jake had a theory he wanted to test out. Something for a more opportune time.

The fight went rather easy, as Jake had predicted. Bertram easily tanked the biggest deer and even an additional one, while Theodore, Jacob, and Dennis took on one each. The final two deer-like things had already been killed or disabled by the initial barrage, making the fight effectively five versus nine, with Jake not participating.

Theodore managed to kill his deer quite easily—it was only level 2—by landing a swipe on its neck, cutting it open. His style was a bit reserved and defensive, but he had a good build and didn't lack confidence. He was also rather good in spotting openings, and Jake was even fairly sure he saw him throw in a feint.

Dennis took a bit longer with his two daggers cutting away at the beast. He was by far the fastest in the group besides Jake, and he also used his active ability, which allowed him to have small bursts of speed here and there. He did hesitate a bit and clearly didn't like fighting, but he got the job done nevertheless.

In Jake's honest opinion, Jacob was the worst combatant in their group by quite a margin. He panicked nearly instantly when the beast got close, and just swung his sword back and forth. The casters did decently, with Joanna having the worst accuracy—which Jake could honestly not blame her for, considering her circumstances. Ahmed was by far the best, having quite the accuracy and aiming for vital spots, with Lina falling somewhere in between.

Caroline had little to do during the actual fight, as her healing skill was touch-based, but she was fast to call out potential dangers and even healed Jacob mid-combat at one point. She was surprisingly good.

Casper was also decent, but Jake was kind of biased when it came to archery. His results did speak for themselves, though, as he did get in some good shots, even taking down one of the deer solo when they first engaged.

The entire ordeal took only a couple of minutes, with the last opponents to die being the big deer that slowly got whittled down by Bertram taking its hits with his shield, and the casters and Casper shooting it to death.

Jake did not get any credits for the kills since he did not actively participate, confirming his suspicions that you had to do damage or contribute in some way in order to earn experience. His moral support and oversight did not seem to count as actual helping.

The gains were also decent. Disregarding TP, they had a couple of level-ups, also resulting in race level-ups. This also truly confirmed the hypothesis that race leveled up every second level in the class.

Without further ado, they moved on and ran into a couple of smaller groups of beasts over the next couple of hours. Jake only had to step in once when a rather large level 7 badger ran past Bertram, heading straight for Lina. However, it was easily killed by Jake with an arrow to one of its legs followed by another that hit the thing in its right eye, likely penetrating the brain as the beast fell dead immediately.

They did sustain some injuries, the most dangerous one being when Theodore took a nasty bite to one arm and had to drink a healing potion. The minor injuries, like scratches and such, were healed by Caroline after every fight. While she could not do much in combat, her healing was invaluable, as it allowed them to always stay in top condition, and healing also seemed to remove any chance of infection in the wound. Assuming that was still a thing. *Oh god... can bacteria get levels?* Jake quickly threw this thought all the way to the back of his mind. *Happy thoughts, happy thoughts...*

While a healing potion could heal injuries too, and in general worked way faster, they seemed to have some kind of cooldown. If you drank one, you couldn't drink one for the next hour. Why this was, they didn't know. Heck, they didn't even know why they knew. Theodore just said that he did right after drinking one. System magic or something. They did not know if there were adverse effects from drinking another or if it just wouldn't work, and quite frankly, no one wanted to test it out.

After another rather tough fight and a round of healing, everyone was getting tired, seeing as they had also passed their fourth hour since they set off in the morning. The last group they killed was a small group of the deer-things again, so they decided to make camp and roast the things over a fire. They also found another small stream nearby, allowing everyone to rehydrate. Jake purposely did not eat or drink anything during this time.

He wanted to test exactly how the health and stamina resources worked, and their relation to daily necessities. He wanted to see if potions—primarily stamina potions— could counteract the need for sleep and sustenance. But that was for a time where he felt any actual hunger or need to sleep.

They sat gathered around a small fire eating the roasted deer that—it had to be mentioned—was quite a bit better than badger meat. It was short-lived, however, as their peaceful break was interrupted when Jake heard what sounded like metal rubbing against metal. He got up from the log he had been sitting on and motioned to the rest of the group to get ready for a potential conflict.

The source of the sounds was soon made clear, as out of the bushes walked a large man in full metal armor identical to Bertram's, also carrying a shield and sword. He was on the older side, in his late forties to early fifties, but his presence did not indicate any weakness due to age.

Quite the group followed him. Jake counted fifteen, with more potentially hiding in the dense foliage behind them. There were mainly warriors, which made sense since half of the basic classes were variants of the class. The rest were casters, with only one archer from what Jake could see, and not a single healer.

Jake made quick eye contact with Jacob, which his former leader instantly understood as he went forward.

While Jake certainly was the strongest in their group when it came to combat, he was likely the weakest when it came to negotiation. And while Jacob sucked in combat, he was top tier when it came to social interactions.

The first one to speak was not Jacob, but the middle-aged warrior.

"Well, hello there—my name is Richard," he said in a friendly voice as he looked over their group, his eyes stopping on Caroline for a second. "We saw the smoke from your fire and decided to investigate—no need to worry. We have no intention of fighting anyone. So, who might you people be?"

The man was quite well-spoken and had a relaxed expression on his face. Looking at the situation, Richard's group had them outnumbered by quite a margin. Jake had no confidence in fighting so many enemies whatsoever if things turned for the worse. If a fight did happen, it would either be a one-sided slaughter or him and his colleagues scattering like the wind, with likely only Jake making it safely away and the others being hunted down one by one. In other words, fighting was out of the question.

"It is good to see other humans at last!" Jacob smiled brightly at the man as he stepped forward. "My name is Jacob, and these are my colleagues from before this so-called tutorial. May I know why you have sought us out? We have no desire for any unnecessary conflicts either."

"Of course not; we humans are meant to stick together!" the man answered with an exaggerated belly-laugh, as he suddenly seemed to turn serious. "My and two other groups, much like yours, have decided to team up in order to get through this purgatory that refers to itself as a tutorial. Of course, we need all the people we can have, so we would love for you and your friends to join us."

Jake noticed how Jacob seemed to instantly catch on to how he used the term "team up." It didn't take a genius to see that only a single leader existed in the group in front of them. Richard might've claimed it was a team-up, but clearly, it was simply assimilation.

Jacob didn't let his thoughts show, but he kept smiling as he nodded. "It's good to hear that other groups are also doing well out there. May I have a talk with my colleagues first? I am sure you understand that a decision like this is best made unanimously."

"Of course! Of course! Take your time!"

Despite Richard's agreement, Jacob was quite clear they were just words. They had to find a solution fast.

Richard motioned for them to stay as his group allowed Jacob to retreat slightly, motioning for Jake and the others to do the same. During it all, Jake kept an eye on the other group in case they tried something. Richard shot a glance at the archer that had been standing at his side from the very beginning, and Jake noticed said archer going slightly forward, clearly intending to listen in with his high Perception. *His second-in-command?*

As they got a small distance away, Jacob turned his back to the other group and addressed them. "What do you guys think of them? A bigger group would be safer, and I think that their offer is...»

He kept talking positively of the offer, but when he looked around, he saw that Jake had knelt down and written some words on the ground with his fingers:

THEY LISTEN
BAD FEELING
CAREFUL

Jacob nodded, looking to have already expected it. That was likely why he kept his true thoughts hidden. Jacob promptly removed the words with his hand, acting like he was just dusting off his shoes. He continued speaking as he received reluctant looks from those around him.

«... But we are familiar with each other, and we seem to function well as a team. There are also certain drawbacks to big groups, such as a higher need for food, and it may end up provoking some of the stronger beasts or something like that."

The others had also seen Jake's scribbles and nodded along to what Jacob said. None of them seemed to like it, probably getting a bad vibe from Richard and his group.

Jake saw the other archer out of the corner of his eye, subtly shaking his head at the middle-aged warrior, who frowned at the seemingly unexpected response. But the archer quickly wiped the frown off his face as he put on another smile and approached their group once more.

"I understand if you are reluctant, but working together is in the best interest of everyone here."

"It certainly is, but—»

At this point, Richard directly turned to Caroline, who stood at the back, and interrupted Jacob. "Young lady, you would not happen to be a healer, would you? It would be greatly appreciated if you came with us."

Caroline looked shocked and confused, but didn't manage to say anything before Richard turned back to Jacob and the rest of them.

"Your colleagues don't have to come, you know? They can, but you could also go with us alone—safety in numbers and all that. I can promise you an appropriate position in our group, and that we will do anything we can to keep you safe. There will, of course, also be levels aplenty. If you just come with us, I am sure we can solve this amicably."

Even Jake, with his horrendous social skills, could interpret the undertone in that one.

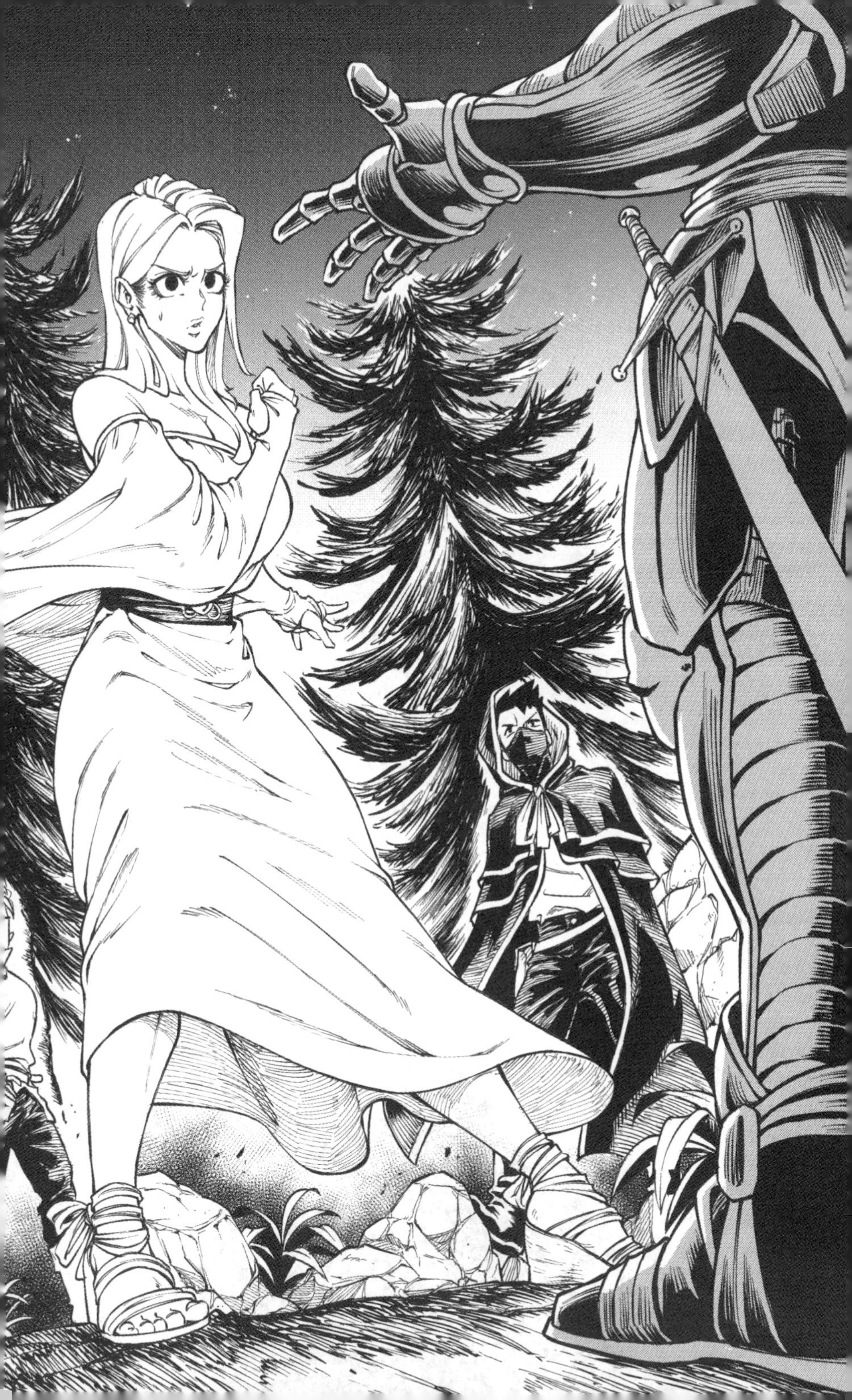

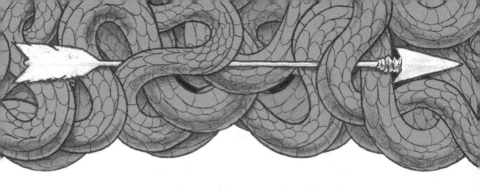

CHAPTER 12
A SPLITTING PROVOCATION

The mood of the conversation shifted, and the smile on Jacob's face was gone. Jake was also working in overdrive, analyzing the situation. Should he take them by surprise and shoot the man? Even if he tried, he had no confidence in landing the shot. And even if it did hit *and* somehow managed to kill him, chances were it would end badly if the other side retaliated, or more accurately, *when* they retaliated, as he seriously doubted they would just take getting their leader killed lying down.

Caroline was also looking incredibly nervous at this point, hiding a bit behind Bertram, who had a stoic look on his face. The situation was tense, to say the least. She did not look at all like she wanted to respond positively to his... "invitation."

Richard looked on as he flashed a light smile, but his eyes were still rather cold. The ones behind him also seemed to have tensed up too and had their hands close to their weapons. He finally started talking again, breaking the silence before they reached a breaking point.

"I'm just going to be honest with you all—healers are scarce in this place. We had one, but he died within an hour of entering the tutorial. Three groups, thirty people, and only one fucking healer." He spat on the ground, clearly frustrated. "So, young lady, I am serious when I say that you would be treated well. We need you far more than you need us."

He turned back to Jacob again and continued.

"You agreed that we humans are meant to stick together, right? We have no healer. We have only a handful of healing potions. There are no medical supplies, no hospital, no doctors, no nothing. Does she not have a responsibility to help her fellow man? I want to solve this peacefully with everyone walking away happy, but I don't exactly have a choice here. We need a healer, one way or another. We only need the healer. The rest of you are free to choose what you want to do.

"Just know that her joining us is nonnegotiable. Not having a healer is just too risky in this place, and I have already lost too many good men and women unnecessarily. If you and your colleagues join us, you will be treated like everyone else. We will make hunting parties based on optimal setups, with the healer joining my own party, naturally. I can even promise that if you don't wish to fight, we offer protection as long as you contribute in other ways. Just think it over carefully."

Richard seemed to be done talking, as he gave them space once more. He had thrown the ball in their court, and now the question was just what to do...

They could try and run, but they were clearly outnumbered, and their levels too low. Jake had a feeling that the majority of the opposing party was at level 5 or above. He said they had run out of healing potions, which indicated that they had done plenty of fighting. *Fighting is off the list.*

The second option was to join them. Jake did not like that option at all. He got a bad feeling from them. He did not doubt that Caroline would remain unharmed, but what about the rest of them? Would they be used as meat-shields or what? They would clearly not allow them to act autonomously for fear of them leaving with Caroline.

The third option was just to hand her over. They would likely let them go, as while humans were worth hunting, they were far more dangerous than beasts in most cases. Additionally, they would have to try and not antagonize Caroline more than necessary. Jake doubted anyone would want a healer who wanted nothing more than to kill the people she healed. Or worse, refuse to heal at all.

Needless to say, Jake was not a fan of just handing her over. One reason was that they would end up with the same issue that Richard's group currently had. He was hesitant to voice his thoughts when Theodore started talking.

"Maybe we should just go with them. Imagine not having access to any kind of healing or medicine in this shithole. It would make even the best desperate. We don't even know them—why are we taking an antagonistic position?"

Quite a few of the group members nodded, while others stayed silent.

Jake could easily see Richard smiling in the other group, clearly approving of the direction their conversation was currently taking. Theodore did have a good point, though—they were clearly desperate. Who were they to reject helping the other group? Without a healer or health potions, a single bite or claw wound could become infected and fester, making even small scratches and injuries fatal.

Jake also thought back to his own objective. He had decided that he wanted to try and help his colleagues learn how to fend for themselves. If they joined a larger group, they would be significantly safer from the beasts.

According to Richard, Caroline, one of the few people Jake actually cared about, would be safe for sure. He did not doubt the middle-aged man when he guaranteed that he would do anything to protect her. Who would be stupid enough to piss off or kill a walking hospital in a forest filled with dangers?

Jake, however, was not at all open to her going alone. It would leave the other eight without a healer. He also had serious doubts that Caroline would ever agree to leave them behind. Especially not Jacob.

As the discussion continued, Richard and his crew patiently waited, and the decision to join was slowly reached. But there were still reservations. How would they be treated? Would they be considered outsiders? What reason would Richard have to keep them around after already getting his hands on Caroline? The predominant fear was that they would be treated more like hostages than members.

Jake had said nothing so far. He had kept silent, listening and taking in the conversation. Richard seemed not to care what they thought as long as they joined. No, Jake needed insurance. He needed something that would keep them safe and treated well.

He had no intention of joining either way. He had decided to go his own way last night already. He needed strength, and he needed power. And he did *need* power. He could feel himself becoming restless from not progressing.

It would be foolish not to grasp an opportunity to rise above what he currently was. More importantly, he also wanted to. He wanted to hunt, fight, and encounter challenges. And he would not be able to do that if he stayed with any group.

Jake thought of his desire to hunt. He thought back to right after he had killed the three attackers the day before, and the feeling of accomplishment and fulfillment—the feeling of power. Basking in the feeling, he channeled his Bloodline as a faux smile of never-ending confidence appeared on his lips.

"Richard, is it? What's your level?" he asked in a calm voice.

Richard looked over at them, truly noticing Jake for the first time. A young, inconspicuous man completely covered in the cloak given out to all archers. He surely saw nothing remarkable until he looked at Jake's face. His eyes were practically glowing, and he had a confident smile, with a trace of excitement hidden deep beneath. Not a single sign of fear or worry evident, almost as if he wanted a fight to break out.

"I am level 9 in my class, and we have a couple of others in our group at level 7 and above," Richard answered truthfully, seemingly not afraid of sharing it.

The ones before him had clearly been office workers or something similar before this tutorial. The only odd one out was Jake, who must have given him a bit of a different feeling.

Either way, they had leveled from entering until now, only resting for a few hours. They had played it safe due to not having a healer, but Richard probably doubted a single individual could outmatch them. He probably also doubted the man was actually strong, as his colleagues couldn't hide their confused looks at how he acted.

"And who might you be? Your level too, if you don't mind?"

Jake looked back at him with a small sigh of disappointment. It was not an act, either. He had genuinely hoped that the man was stronger. From what he had seen, level 10 seemed to be a power spike for monsters, and humans might experience something similar.

"Well, that's slightly disappointing. I was hoping for you to be stronger," Jake said. "As for my name and level? I am Mr. Eat Shit, and I am level go-fuck-yourself."

Richard's smile faded significantly. Jacob, Caroline, and all the others were gobsmacked at what the hell Jake was doing, openly provoking the man. Especially how Jake kept up that weird, daring demeanor, despite them being outnumbered so badly.

"I thought we were close to reaching an agreement here?" Richard asked, more than a little annoyed at the unexpected development. Who was this archer that he hadn't even bothered noticing before? What gave him confidence?

"Oh, fairly sure they're joining you, but I am not," Jake said, still smiling at the man as he walked closer to Richard and his camp. "I have bigger prey to hunt." As he got closer, he felt a prickling sensation making him aware of the danger lurking behind the man. He distinctly felt three archers who likely had their bows aimed at him in case he tried something.

"I just wanted to make something clear," he continued. "I will leave my former colleagues to you, so do take proper care of them. Of course, if something happens, we will have issues." By now, he was only a single step away from the middle-aged warrior.

Richard was a good ten centimeters taller than Jake, literally looking down on the archer. Yet he seemed unsure of how to act.

"Huh, issues? What kind of issues would those be?" He squinted down at Jake while taking half a step forward to tower over him.

Jake's smile widened. "The kind of issues where I get convenient prey served on a silver platter. Do you believe yourself superior? Do you think those three archers will land their shot before I remove your head? Do you think their arrows have any chance of hitting? Do you honestly think that you are the predator in this scenario?"

Jake opened his arms wide out to the sides, watching Richard tense up as he dropped the smile and turned serious. "Because you're not. You can take them, train with them, fight with them, and survive with them. But I will be watching. A single misstep, and I will hunt you and all your pals down one by one. Sweet dreams."

Jake turned around and started walking away.

In his sphere, he saw the archer that stood just behind Richard had begun drawing his bow, but Richard raised a hand indicating for him to stop. Jake made the exact same motion. The other men appeared stunned by the revelation that he could still see them with his back turned.

Jake walked back to his colleagues, who stood there looking confused.

"You are leaving us?" Casper managed to mutter out.

"Yeah, it was my plan all along. I have my own goals for this tutorial. If you join them, you should have a much higher chance of surviving than on your own. Don't worry, I will check in occasionally." Jake gave them a smile. Not the threatening, borderline maniac smile that he had given Richard, but a friendly one. "Do take diligent care of everyone, Jacob, and don't let them bully you or anyone else."

Then he turned toward the forest, intending to leave.

"Wait!" Jacob called out and ran up to him, hugging him and covertly passing him one of the satchels he had been carrying. One contained all the health potions from the attackers last night as well as Jacob's own three health and stamina potions.

Finishing the hug and distancing himself, Jacob looked at Jake and smiled. "Take care out there, my friend, and please do come back and check in whenever you can."

Jake nodded and walked away from their camp. There was no heartfelt goodbye from any of them, except Casper, who yelled to take care. He had a strong feeling he wouldn't see them for quite a while, but even without showing himself, he hoped the power of the threat would remain. However, he was pretty sure that dear Richard would give him an opportunity to truly hammer it home soon.

He had seen Richard whisper something to the archer as Jake walked back to his colleagues earlier. Looking over once more, he saw said archer—whom he had guessed to be his second-in-command—now gone, along with some of the light warriors.

Jake smiled as he entered the bushes and walked at a brisk pace directly away from the clearing. He could not see them anywhere in his sphere, but he knew they were coming. Richard did not strike him as a man who took threats very well, and sending a team after him to remove a potential threat was perfectly in character.

Picking up the pace, he started sprinting to create some distance. His heart was still pumping from his acting before. He didn't quite know how he had found the confidence to do that, but in some ways, wasn't there a thrill in that kind of challenge too?

Excitement bubbled up in his stomach as he found a spot that was simply *perfect*.

He smiled as he thought of his pursuers. They would arrive soon, he felt it. He started retracing his path for ten or so meters by stepping in his old footsteps, approaching a tree. He had purposely walked close to it on his way here for this reason, after all.

Moving in accordance with his basic stealth skill, he felt it activate as he quickly climbed the tree and found a good hiding spot among the leaves. Soon they would be upon him, and he was ready for them. Thoughts about how they were human beings didn't enter his mind even for a second. Today, they were simply prey.

They seem to have misunderstood something, he thought as he waited. *I am the one hunting them.*

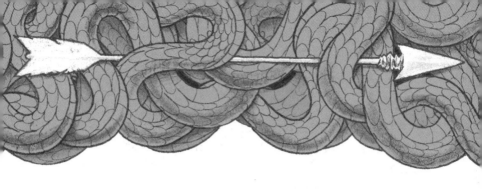

CHAPTER 13
NICHOLAS (1/2)

How troublesome, Nicholas thought as he pursued the archer on Richard's orders.

Nicholas, an archer himself, was silently running through the forest with six of his companions. Four archers and three light warriors made up the hunting party. In his opinion, it was total overkill to send seven men for a single archer from some corporate office.

Seriously, what the fuck was up with that guy? Spewing off some cliché bullshit to look like a badass? He'd had to hold himself back from cringing during the entire thing, and had barely managed to not just shoot him in the back as he walked off.

Sadly, Richard didn't want to spoil the relationship with their new healer. While the guy did do some weird stuff, it was nothing to make Nicholas wary of him. It was totally unnecessary to send so many, but Richard was nothing if not thorough.

Ultimately, he did, of course, understand why Richard sent people after him. Either he was a real and serious threat, or he was a lunatic, in which case he would be a chaotic threat. In both cases, the issue was best nipped in the bud.

Nicholas himself had been one of the people who'd entered the tutorial with Richard, and he'd worked for the man before the initiation. Richard ran a private security firm and had employees contracted in several offices in their city of operation. Nicholas was just another faceless employee, but his track record had earned him some amount of trust, which had netted him the right-hand man's position in this tutorial.

Finding a healer was fortunate. Having none was quite honestly hell, especially for the warriors who often got minor injuries, being forced to be in melee and all that. They'd had a healer when they first got here, but he'd gotten impaled by a huge stag in one of their first fights. This left them with only a limited amount of healing potions, made worse by having to waste them on what a healer could fix in minutes for just a bit of mana.

Even luckier was that the healer was a part of a team of laymen who were clearly inexperienced when it came to battle. And yet he had been asked by his boss to pursue some archer with a big mouth who decided to play cool. He did not buy the guy's bullshit at all.

He personally wanted to just bet on the guy getting himself killed, but Richard was not the kind of man you rejected. He was their leader, with pretty much everyone just calling him "boss." The title hadn't been earned through nepotism or posturing, but sheer competence.

Nicholas didn't question his decision, but it did suck a bit that they had to take in a group of weaklings. He doubted a single one of them was even level 5. At least the healer chick looked nice, and the red-haired caster was quite good too. The one he found the most annoying was that crippled middle-aged woman—the very definition of a burden in his opinion.

I am sure Richard will find some way to fix it, he thought. How would they be to blame if the newbies had unfortunate accidents during combat? As long as they could get the healer on their side, all were fair game.

They had been running for a while and finally reached the area where Mr. Bigmouth had entered the forest. They all entered stealth, as they had a rule that every archer and light warrior had to pick stealth at level 5. Richard wanted a strong scouting force and, as this situation proved, assassination team.

They snuck through the underbrush as they scouted ahead. The guy had not exactly been sneaky, leaving clear footsteps in the underbrush. While none of them had a tracking skill, it did not mean that tracking was impossible. You just had to do it the old-fashioned way.

As they followed the footsteps, they suddenly seemed to stop in the middle of a small clearing.

Before any of them could react, Nicholas heard something pierce through the wind, followed by a thud. The light warrior at his side fell over with an arrow stuck in the back of his head, dead as dead can be.

WHAT THE FUCK!? was his immediate internal reaction as he acted.

"TAKE COVER!" he yelled as he ran for the trees, quickly hiding behind one. Peeking back into the clearing, he saw two corpses. One of the archers was now also dead, shot during their retreat. *What the fuck is going on!?*

He activated Archer's Eye and started looking up at the trees. He had a feeling their attacker was up in one of those, and it didn't take long before he spotted the enemy. It was another archer, based on the fact that another arrow flew out from a tree crown.

Nicholas nocked an arrow and went out from behind the tree, firing at where the arrow had come from. He got no feedback from his shot as he quickly backed behind the tree once more. He peeked around it again, his high Perception and skill both working on overdrive.

Before he found anything, he heard another scream. He charged over to where the scream had come from, dashing between trees. Arriving at the location, he saw a wounded archer with an arrow in his chest—luckily, he was still alive. Nicholas quickly ripped the arrow out and took out his last health potion, making the man drink it.

The wound visibly healed, and the now healing archer opened his mouth: "I got a shot in," he barely managed to say, still heaving for breath as his lungs healed. "In the stomach, I think."

The man fell, still out of breath, while the potion did its magic. Nicholas left the man to lick his wounds as he heard more yelling from his comrades all around him.

Jake was still smiling to himself as he examined the arrow in his stomach. He considered ripping it out and drinking a healing potion, but his health had only gone down a measly 50 points. Not even one sixth of his total health after his new title. Ripping it out would only make it bleed more, making him lose more health, and quite frankly, it barely affected him. It hurt like hell, but it was more than manageable.

His initial ambush had gone well, killing two of them right off the bat. He also felt the sensation of level-ups, but he decided to ignore the system messages for now. It wasn't the time to get distracted.

However, the third target he had gone for had been prepared and had been outside his sphere when they spotted each other, resulting in them both landing an arrow on the other. Jake had narrowly missed the man's heart, but still landed a fatal blow. If the man did not have any healing potions, he would bleed out in minutes. Or drown in his own blood as it filled up his lungs. Jake wasn't a doctor, but he was pretty sure it would be one or the other.

From the bush he was now hiding in, he focused on his sphere as he moved out, sneaking in between trees. He saw a lone light warrior hidden behind a tree in his sphere, the tree itself posing no obstacle to his Perception ability. His initial plan had worked out perfectly, baiting all of them into the middle of a small clearing and then attacking, making them split to all sides. Divide and conquer and all that.

Jake threw a small rock to the left of the warrior as he approached from the right. The man turned instantly toward the sound, and Jake promptly charged forth, sliding up behind him, putting his left hand across the man's mouth, and using his right to slit his throat. The man managed to slash his dagger backwards in an awkward last-ditch effort, hitting Jake in his left shoulder.

The man went limp, with Jake holding him until he got the notification. When it came, he let the corpse go as he looked at the knife wound on his left shoulder. It hurt, but the knife had barely done any damage, and he could still easily use it.

Three, maybe four down. At least three to go, including the archer leading them.

He had seen the archer in charge of their little assassination troop. He was fast, faster than Jake, indicating that he had a higher level. And not by a little either. Jake estimated the man to be at least level 7 or 8.

Jake began sneaking toward his next target as he tried to stay hidden. He had already decided to leave one alive to send a message if possible, but it sure as hell was not going to be their leader.

He had already spotted the one he wanted to function as his messenger. It was a young archer, no more than seventeen or eighteen. Jake was looking at him at this moment and could both see and feel him shake in fear. He kept throwing glances toward the clearing where the two corpses were.

Jake decided to ignore the kid and instead started looking for another target. From the way the kid had frozen up, Jake saw no scenario where he would prove an issue.

Jake felt no one in his sphere as he moved, nor did he see anything. He closed his eyes and focused on his hearing. At first, he heard nothing but the ambient sound of the wind and the occasional beast or bird, until he picked up another, more relevant sound—labored breathing.

He silently snuck toward the sound of the breathing, and soon the last light warrior entered his Sphere of Perception. Unlike the others, this one had decided to cover himself in leaves and parts of the underbrush, practically invisible in combination with the basic stealth skill as he lay prone on the ground. Jake doubted he would even be able to spot him using Archer's Eye.

Luckily, Jake did not need his eyes to see him. The man was hidden well if you looked at him, but with an omnidirectional sphere, what he was doing barely counted as hiding. Jake decided to get a vertical advantage and climbed a tree to ensure his attack would prove lethal.

From up there, he had a clear shot right at the man. He sure had done a decent job hiding, as Jake could not even spot him from above, mainly due to him lying completely still. Jake nocked an arrow and drew his bow, aiming for the head.

He found it interesting how not a single of the basic outfits for any of the classes provided any protection for the head. Even the heavy warriors didn't have a helmet, despite their otherwise full armor. The only thing remotely close were the hoods on the cloaks that casters, healers, and archers had. But that did not exactly provide a lot of protection against an arrow.

The only true protection seemed to be provided by the Toughness stat, maybe Vitality, and perhaps Endurance to some extent? He did not know exactly, but he did remember the light warrior class not offering any stat points to Toughness and only one to Vitality. In other words, their level advantage meant little to nothing if hit, except for maybe one or two levels in race.

Which was exactly what led to the hidden warrior dying without even knowing how. All that was left was what looked like a stack of leaves and branches with an arrow sticking out it. A red liquid slowly soaked the underbrush around the arrow.

Jake confirmed the system notification of him getting the kill, and checked his list of notifications quickly, finding only 4. Meaning that the archer he'd traded arrows with earlier still lived. *Must have used a health potion*, he thought.

He decided to go finish off the archer, doubting he had gotten far. While a healing potion did renew the lost health points instantly, it still took a bit of time for the body to fully mend, and judging from where he had landed the arrow, the guy was hopefully still down for the count.

Jake climbed down from the tree and snuck toward where he had fought the archer. He still had to be careful with the leader of the hit squad on the loose. The guy had decent skill, judging by his fast reactions to the initial ambush, and his accuracy was quite decent according to his return shot.

He quickly found the archer, who had done nothing more than drag himself to the other side of the tree Jake had left him at. He was still heaving for breath, as his lungs had just finished healing, and was not in any condition to put up a proper fight.

While it was not exactly exciting prey, an enemy was an enemy. The archer had covered his body and face with his cloak and made sure that blood was clearly visible as he tried to sit completely still, likely hoping to fool Jake into believing he was already dead.

Jake was off to the side of the man, still sneaking, as he drew his bow. The man had his vision blocked by his hood, completely unaware as death approached.

Jake aimed and fired the arrow. The moment he released the arrow, his danger sense went ballistic, and he barely managed to move a bit to the side as an arrow entered his sphere and struck him in the back. A wave of immense pain washed over him, making him grit his teeth. He barely managed to stumble behind a nearby tree, narrowly dodging yet another arrow.

He slumped down behind the tree and quickly ripped out the arrow still in his stomach, then the one in his back. The one in the stomach was narrow, only penetrating muscle mostly, but the one in the back had hit something important. He quickly drank a healing potion and felt a cold sensation spread throughout his body. The potion itself was tasteless, like water—not that he had any time to think about flavors at the moment.

He couldn't help but smile to himself despite the pain as he confirmed the kill notification for the already-wounded archer. Afterward, he quickly opened his status page and threw all his Free Points into Perception. He didn't even have time to look at his stats before his danger sense acted up again, as he had to slide around the tree, avoiding another arrow.

His smile grew wider as he got to temporary safety once more. The archer was outside his sphere, despite it becoming slightly stronger from the increased Perception given during his level-ups and the allocated Free Points.

Whoever this leader was, he wasn't an amateur. He knew his way around a bow, and unlike many others, he didn't hesitate. Jake felt the excitement practically boil in his stomach as he felt his wounds heal. Finally, he had found a worthwhile opponent. His terrible taunt and equally terrible acting had been one hundred percent worth it.

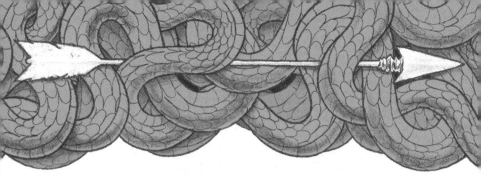

Chapter 14
Nicholas (2/2)

Nicholas did feel slightly regretful sacrificing his comrade in order to get the drop on the archer. Not because his former ally died, but because he had failed in killing the enemy. After he had given the wounded archer a healing potion, he'd decided to hide in a tree twenty or so meters away, with a clear line of sight to the wounded man.

In other words, he had set up his ally as bait.

The enemy archer seemed to have a Perception skill of some kind, or something that achieved a similar effect. It was a way of locating nearby individuals at the minimum. He first thought it was perhaps the Basic Tracking skill, but he had also seen the archer use Basic Stealth. Which would either mean that the man had unlocked two skills, hence being above level 10, or had some other means he was unaware of.

Ultimately, it did not matter. What mattered was killing the bastard, and his trap had worked like a charm until the very last moment.

As he timed his shot with the enemy archer's, the man reacted as if he had eyes in his back, and managed to slightly swerve to the side, lessening the damage from the shot significantly. Nicholas cursed to himself as he shot another arrow, but once more, the man stumbled to the side, dodging without even turning around. Before he could fire another shot, the guy had already fled to safety behind a tree.

He jumped down from the tree he had been in and started running to the side while still keeping a good distance. He spotted the archer once more and quickly shot another arrow, but once more, he managed to slip around the tree.

What followed was a cat-and-mouse game, where Nicholas kept shooting arrows whenever he saw the other archer as he slowly got closer. Based on the movements of the other archer, he must have consumed a health potion, putting Nicholas on a timer before he would be back in top condition.

The entire thing was frustrating, and only got worse as the other archer started returning fire. Neither of them seemed inclined to enter melee range, and with a good twenty meters still between them, they entered a standstill.

Not that Nicholas feared entering a melee bout. As a part of his job before the initiation, he'd received training in hand-to-hand, and his skills with a knife were not to be scoffed at. While he'd had limited experience with a bow before the tutorial, the system had even given him a rank upgrade to his one-handed weapon skill once. He had picked Archer because he believed a ranged weapon would be superior to a melee one, despite light warrior perhaps suiting him better in retrospect.

Jake felt quite a bit better after avoiding a couple more arrows, and he even started shooting back. His life was in danger at every moment, and he had a couple of close shaves on account of the other archer being both faster and stronger than him. He was enjoying every moment of it.

They both dodged and weaved in between trees, firing arrows back and forth, neither finding any luck. Jake was absolutely fine with this stalemate, as he started to feel better and better, his high Vitality helping to heal his internal injuries.

Despite a healing potion's magical effect of restoring health points, it did not instantly fix the body. That was all up to the person's Vitality—a stat that Jake had no lack of due to his [Bloodline Patriarch] title.

As they shot at each other, they ended up slowly moving closer together. The initial twenty meters became fifteen and then only ten. With less than twenty arrows remaining, the other archer finally entered Jake's Sphere of Perception, making the physical barriers between them far less relevant, as he no longer needed to rely purely on sight.

The forest was quite a sight at this moment, with tens of trees having arrows stuck in them. Some were low on the trunk, while others were closer to their tops, as the two archers had periodically climbed them in order to get any advantage.

Jake could feel the other archer becoming more and more frustrated throughout the fight, and when he entered his sphere, Jake finally confirmed the big frown on the man's face.

Jake smiled to himself as he called out, "This is fun, right?"

"What the fuck do you want?" the other archer yelled back.

"A name, I would prefer. Name's Jake!"

"And why would I care about that?" the other man once more yelled, clearly not enjoying their exchange whatsoever.

Jake saw that the man was spending his time conjuring more arrows. Not that he had much to say, as Jake was doing exactly the same. The other archer, however, was down to only eleven arrows, with Jake still having nineteen. Based on the other archer's skill level, he had likely counted them and knew he was at a disadvantage, leading him to endure the conversation to buy time.

"It would be a shame to just end up as another random notification of experience and tutorial points gained, wouldn't it?" Jake replied honestly.

The other man had skill, to be sure. Despite his clear frustration with the situation, he still kept his cool and had a methodical approach, never losing control of his emotions enough to hamper his performance. This would not be Jake's last fight with life and death on the line against a strong enemy, but he wanted to know the name of his first, at least. He slightly regretted not getting the name of the three assailants he had first killed, but the situation had not exactly called for a name exchange.

"Still trying to act cool, huh?" he sneered back. "Get a grip; you are making me cringe over here. But if you care so much, then my name is Nicholas."

"Well, nice to meet you, I guess. Was my taunt really that bad?" Jake had tried to make himself seem like a total badass, but, thinking back, it came off more as him acting like a fifteen-year-old's version of a badass.

"Cringeworthy enough to make me want to get rid of you, even without Richard ordering it. Seriously, what the fuck was that?"

"Seriously, that bad? I guess I should apologize?" Jake was more than a little embarrassed. *Never going to do anything like that again. Ever.*

"Still going to kill you," Nicholas answered. "You fucked up really bad, you know. Making an enemy out of us. Do you really think your friends will be safe after I kill you and return to tell how full of shit you were?"

"Okay, I guess this means the talk is over," Jake muttered as much to himself as Nicholas.

The conversation at this point would lead nowhere, but Jake was happy enough that he got a name to call his opponent. Jake exited from behind the tree and jumped to the side, shooting another arrow at Nicholas, who managed to dodge it quite easily.

The purpose of the shot had only been to interrupt his opponent's conjuration of arrows.

The game of shooting back and forth resumed, but Nicholas seemed to quickly notice his disadvantage at the closer range, as he seemed to pick up on Jake knowing his position despite having no line of sight. They were close enough that they ended up grazing each other here and there, but nothing even close to lethal.

Jake's opponent hesitated for a bit as he hid behind a tree. In the end, the man appeared to decide he would be far more exposed trying to run, and even if he did manage to get away, it would achieve very little.

Nicholas, instead of running away or getting more distance, decided to close the gap.

The enemy archer ran back and forth between the trees, and while the distance was only reduced by inches at a time as they kept shooting back and forth, the man did make constant advances toward Jake.

Jake, on the other hand, was fine with the other archer deciding to get closer. While he most certainly preferred ranged combat, he was not afraid to meet the enemy in melee. Not because he had any confidence in his abilities with a melee weapon, but because he unconditionally trusted his instincts at this point. They were not perfect, and he had taken several wounds during the fight, but they were nevertheless extremely reliable.

He suddenly got an idea as something appeared in his sphere while dodging yet another arrow. He kept dodging toward a certain tree while returning fire at opportune times.

Finally, he got to the particular tree he had been aiming for, having increased the distance to a good eight to ten meters once more. He dodged behind the tree as Nicholas followed close behind. It was at this tree that Jake had killed the wounded archer at the beginning of the battle.

During the course of combat, they had moved around so much that they eventually switched locations from where they had started, as they'd both circled the forest from tree to tree. This meant that Nicholas could not see the dead archer from where he was now hiding. Jake, on the other hand, stood behind the tree, right next to the fresh corpse.

Jake once more smirked as he hoisted up the dead archer, leaning him against the tree in preparation. He then got out from behind the tree, firing yet another arrow. Jake purposely stayed around this tree as Nicholas finally got within a couple of meters.

Nicholas charged for Jake as he circled the tree where Jake had set the trap. As he got around it, he lunged with no hesitation and stabbed for the throat. Jake saw Nicholas smile as his knife sank into the flesh of his dead comrade. His smile quickly disappeared, however, as the man noticed the face of his opponent.

What instead met him were the dead eyes of the comrade he had sacrificed earlier. Before he could process what had happened, a knife came out from behind the corpse, as Jake penetrated his chest.

With a cough of blood, Nicholas fell backward, the knife being ripped out in the process. Blood poured out, and Jake knew his heart had been hit and that he was done for as blood filled the fallen archer's mouth.

Jake looked down at the man, who was collapsed on the soft underbrush of the forest, his eyes still open as he struggled in vain. His Vitality had spared him from an otherwise instant kill, as his health points were nearly depleted.

"Good fight," Jake stated solemnly.

"Fuck y—" Nicholas tried to say as he coughed up more blood. He didn't attempt to speak again before the final vestige of life left him.

Jake sighed as he got the notification confirming the kill. He went forward and closed the man's—no, Nicholas'—eyes.

At one point, he had considered cutting off the head of this leader to send a message to Richard that his threat was serious, but he could not bring himself to defile the corpse of someone who had given him the best fight of his life. It would also be just a bit too cliché.

Jake instead decided to bury his fallen opponent's corpse, but first, he had some unfinished business with the last member of the hunting party. He walked toward where the archer had been frozen in fear and found him still in the same place, clearly attempting to hide.

He had no respect for this young man, only pity. He was barely an adult, if one at all, and he had been thrown into this messed-up tutorial with beasts, monsters, and people out to kill him. People like Jake.

The kid's attempt to hide was rendered rather pointless by his constant shivering, making it easy to find him even without Jake's sphere. The kid had his dagger in his hand, hidden under the cloak, but he had either lost or thrown away his bow at some point.

As Jake got closer, the archer started shaking even more, and finally summoned the courage to look up, only to see Jake in a blood-red cloak that had once been brown. Before the kid managed to scream, Jake ran forward and easily disarmed him by giving him a solid punch in the gut, making him keel over. His knife dropped to the ground.

"Your pals are dead, kid," Jake said as he looked at the kid, who was clearly thinking that he was going to die. "Return to Richard and say that Nicholas fought well, and do remind him that I was serious when I told him that I would kill him if he does anything to my friends. Oh, and say that he is free to send more people after me. I enjoyed it."

The kid looked up with terror and hesitated at Jake's words. The man in front of him was, in his eyes, a monster in human skin. Out of nowhere, two of his friends had died, and as he'd been getting his bearings, he'd heard panicked screams all around him.

He had frozen up, not daring to move as he feared yet another arrow would come out of nowhere and end his life without him even knowing how. He instead hoped—no, begged—that the others would win and come get him. But now everyone was dead, including the seemingly invincible Nicholas, who even the super-scary Richard respected as his equal. Worse yet, now this monster was standing right in front of him.

"Hello?" Jake wondered aloud as the kid just stood there, shivering. Hadn't he heard him?

The kid tensed up before he quickly began running haphazardly, nearly falling over during his first couple of steps, until he got his bearings and started sprinting.

Jake was a bit confused for a moment, then just shook his head. It looked more than a little silly as the kid bumped into several trees, running like the devil was chasing him.

When the archer left his line of sight, Jake finally slumped down to the ground, tired as hell. It turned out that fighting someone to the death for the better part of an hour was exhausting.

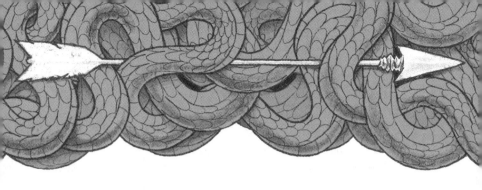

CHAPTER 15
DIVERGING PATHS

As Jake was relaxing, he reflected on how weird stamina was. He was not tired per se, as he did not feel like taking a nap, and his muscles did not ache or anything like that. He had not felt even a second of exhaustion during the fight itself, and yet the second the battle was done, he'd felt drained.

It was likely just mental exhaustion over physical exhaustion, now that he was thinking about it. There was no stat for that. *Or does Willpower help with that?* Naturally, he didn't know, so he could only guess, but since he hadn't really felt less mentally taxed even with the stat increases, he felt like it didn't.

It did kind of make sense that it was tiring to focus on interpreting the feelings from his Sphere of Perception all the time while also being under constant pressure. At the moment, it was still active, vaguely making him aware of everything within eight meters or so, but he was not really directly using it. He couldn't really put it into words, but he guessed one would say it had an "active" and a "passive" mode.

Not that he had any clue how it worked. He just knew what was within it. He did not expressly "see" anything; he just knew the shapes and sizes of everything. It would take a lot of experimentation to truly figure out if it was even possible ever to do so, and for some reason, Jake doubted he would get any answers from just sitting there. Instead, he decided to go through his system notifications and level-ups. And boy, were there notifications.

You have slain [Human (G) - lvl 3 / Warrior (Light) - lvl 6] – Bonus experience earned for killing an enemy above your level. 365 TP earned

You have slain [Human (G) - lvl 2 / Archer - lvl 5] – Experience earned. 243 TP earned

You have slain [Human (G) - lvl 3 / Warrior (Light) - lvl 7] – Bonus experience earned for killing an enemy above your level. 471 TP earned

'DING!' Class: [Archer] has reached level 6 – Stat points allocated, +1 Free Point

'DING!' Race: [Human (G)] has reached level 3 - Stat points allocated, +1 Free Point

You have slain [Human (G) - lvl 3 / Warrior (Light) - lvl 6] – Experience earned. 394 TP earned

You have slain [Human (G) - lvl 3 / Archer - lvl 7] – A small amount of bonus experience earned for killing an enemy with a class above your class level. 654 TP earned

*You have slain [Human (G) - lvl 4 / Archer -

lvl 9] – Bonus experience earned for killing an enemy above your level. 1167 TP earned*

'DING!' Class: [Archer] has reached level 7 – Stat points allocated, +1 Free Point

The gains were good, and he was especially surprised to see that Nicholas had been level 9 with quite a lot of tutorial points too, indicating that he had indeed killed a lot of beasts. He was strong, after all. It made Jake wonder if Richard had lied when he said that he was level 9, but it was honestly inconsequential for now.

He only had a single Free Point left from the last level-up, as midway through the fight, he'd thrown all his points into Perception. Perception was, without a doubt, the stat that he liked the most, and he felt like it had great synergy with his Bloodline ability. Based on that, he decided just to drop his one Free Point into Perception as he opened his newly upgraded status menu.

Status
Name: Jake Thayne
Race: [Human (G) – lvl 3]
Class: [Archer – lvl 7]
Profession: N/A
Health Points (HP): 257/340
Mana Points (MP): 88/140
Stamina: 151/210
Stats
Strength: 21
Agility: 22
Endurance: 21
Vitality: 34
Toughness: 13
Wisdom: 14
Intelligence: 14

Perception: 37
Willpower: 12
Free Points: 0

Once more, he confirmed the weirdness of the Endurance stat. Due to the level-ups, his maximum stamina had increased by 40, making his current also increase by 40. Which ultimately led to him having more stamina than when he'd begun the fight. He also decided to check the tutorial panel now that he was fiddling with menus.

Tutorial Panel
Duration: 63 days & 2:27:39
Total Survivors Remaining: 987/1200
TP Collected: 4629

So many people have died, and not even the first day has passed, he thought. Two hundred and thirteen people dead, more than one-sixth of the total amount of those who had entered the tutorial. Not that Jake had helped that statistic in any way, being personally responsible for nine of those deaths.

He had no clue if his TP was a lot or a little, but according to the rules, he got half the TP of people he killed, so he assumed it had to be a lot. If Nicholas had given him 1167, he would have had double that at 2334, which was still only a bit over half of what he currently had. Not that he had any idea what those damn points could be used for quite yet.

His amount of points was rather respectable, though, as Nicholas had been level 9, while Jake was only level 7. But it did kind of make sense, as he took the accumulated points of people who had killed plenty of enemies to get to their levels. He also had no clue exactly how much TP different enemies gave. He had gotten over 300 from the level 10 boar, and that had been a shared kill.

For the badgers, he'd gotten 4 points from the level 3 ones, and 8 from the level 4 one. The sample size was way too small, but maybe the points just doubled for every level? Though that seemed insane. It did kind of fit with a level 10 boar giving a total of 512, and him getting 300 plus of that on a shared kill.

But that would mean a level 11 beast would give 1024, a level 12 2048, then 4096, and so on. It just seemed way too extreme to work like that. A level 20 beast would give a whopping 524,288 points, which was just absolutely insane if true. Granted, he had no idea how strong a level 20 beast would be, but he doubted they would warrant such a huge point increase.

Once more, he shook his head at his useless internal thoughts. It was a waste of time to think about, and he would just have to go hunt beasts to find out how many points each level gave easily.

He closed all his menus and got up feeling refreshed in both mind and body despite only relaxing for ten minutes. He walked over to Nicholas' body. Jake could still see the unwillingness on his face, but nothing could be done about that. They had fought, and Jake had come out on top.

He had already resolved himself to give a respectable sendoff to the man, but had quickly met the obstacle of not having anything to dig with. He refused to leave the man's body for a bunch of overgrown badgers or deer to eat, so just leaving the body out in the open was not an option. Logically, it was a waste of time, but one could not always remain logical.

He instead decided to make a small fire. Fire was rather easy to make by creating sparks with two daggers, one of which he had taken from one of the dead archers. It was in no way a glorious pyre, but it got the job done. He watched solemnly as the corpse burned, nodding toward what had once been a powerful enemy as the flames consumed it.

Despite being in the same place for a couple of hours while preparing and burning the body, no one showed up. Jake guessed that Richard had decided not to send any more would-be assassins after him for now.

With him being done there, he went to a nearby river and washed himself and his cloak. He bathed in full clothes, his dress shirt and pants still on. The only thing he took off was his shoes and socks, as getting them wet somehow seemed too much.

After cleaning himself and returning his cloak to more brown than red, he decided to set out once more and finally get his solo hunting underway. Excited to get started, he smiled and ran into the depths of the forest once more, like a child entering an amusement park.

Richard had sent off Nicholas and the other fighters with the stealth skill nearly an hour ago. They knew to return to their original camp once the job was done, and he had nearly expected to meet them there. It took a good forty minutes to walk with the newbies to their camp, arriving with little hassle along the way.

The situation was kind of awkward as they walked, but Richard had talked to the young man named Jacob and found him to be rather competent. He was good at reading people, and his group of survivors clearly listened to him and respected him. He was protective of them, but Richard only saw that as a bonus. Despite only interacting with the young man for a bit over half an hour, he had already come to have a modicum of respect for him.

The only thing he was annoyed at was the lack of information he got on the archer he had sent Nicholas after.

Jacob claimed that he had been their coworker before the initiation, and that was about it. He seemed to barely know the guy. The only thing he knew was that he was good with a bow and that he tended to like being alone. It was annoying, but ultimately, it mattered little, as the archer was likely already dead by the time the point was discussed.

Or at least he assumed he was. But the lack of the kill squad who'd gone after him made him worried. The young man had been self-confident to the level of being ridiculous, and Richard was starting to fear that it had not all been bravado. Most of it had been, without a doubt, as he was pretty sure he remembered one of his lines being from a movie, but the paranoia still crept up on him.

Losing a member or two would be more than annoying. They had poured quite a few resources into them after all, raising them all to at least level 5. He had not for a second considered them being wiped out.

Nicholas was too good for that, in his opinion. He was at the same level as himself, and Richard had no confidence in fighting the man head-on. He'd been strong before the tutorial, and in here, he was only stronger. He did have a small fear that Nicholas would one day turn on him, but it did not seem too probable so far. Either way, he saw no scenario in which that arrogant bastard of an archer survived.

Arriving at their small camp with the newbies, the new arrivals looked about, with Richard nodding at the progress in his absence. The camp was basic, to say the least, but they had started constructing some makeshift huts using sticks and leaves, with some grander buildings already being planned. If they had to spend over two months here, they would have to make safe shelter eventually, and no time was better than the present.

After waiting another quarter of an hour, he saw someone running toward the camp, and he didn't immediately recognize him. A haggard teenager with cuts and bruises all over stumbled out the trees, making him get a better look. At first, Richard was happy, as he recognized him as one of Nicholas' men, but soon frowned as he noticed him being alone.

Getting a closer look, he saw the pure terror still present on the face of the youth. Richard instantly turned serious as several questions quickly popped up in his head. Could they have met a dangerous beast out there? Another group? Where was Nicholas?

He took a brisk walk toward the kid and practically collided with him. Before the kid could open his mouth, Richard cut him off:

"What happened? Where is Nicholas? Where the hell is the rest of your squad?"

«D... dead," the kid barely managed to stammer out.

Richard momentarily froze. "Did Nicholas kill them?" he asked. If Nicholas had betrayed him...

«He... died...»

"WHAT!?" Richard screamed, clearly scaring the already-terrified kid. The kid barely managed to explain in bits and pieces how they had gotten into a fight and killed off, but Richard interrupted him. "If he killed everyone," Richard yelled, taking a deep breath as he looked down on the kid, "then why the fuck are you alive?"

At this point, the other people in the camp had noticed the commotion, including Jacob, who Richard noticed got closer to listen in. He knew that Jacob was aware he had sent people after Jake and had hoped that his friend could somehow get away. It was an open secret that no one talked about.

Richard did notice the man honestly looked unsure whether he should be happy or not that his friend had killed a bunch of people. This did at least confirm to Richard that Jacob had not been lying about his lack of comprehension of that archer's skills.

The young archer before him, on the other hand, was nearly pissing himself at this point. He gritted his teeth and explained what had happened in more detail. How they had been ambushed, and two people had died as all they could do was try and get to cover. He told everything he knew, leaving out only the fact that he had hidden cowardly for the entire thing.

"He left me alive because he wanted me to deliver a message," the archer said. "He told me that Nicholas fought well... and that he was serious about what he said earlier."

The teenager looked like he left out something because he was scared, perhaps afraid Richard would get more furious with him. It didn't help as Richard was still fuming nonetheless. He was red in his face but, at the same time, very hesitant about what exactly to do. He looked at the kid, who, in turn, looked like he was contemplating if he should say something.

"What else? Spit it out!" he said, staring angrily.

"Boss... he was not normal. He... he enjoyed it... Smiled while covered in blood... A monster."

Richard was taken aback. He would normally yell more at the kid, but what he saw before him was not just a scared kid, but someone utterly terrified. Reprimanding him would do no good. He instead turned to Jacob, who stood not far away.

Jacob also looked shocked at what he heard, especially the last part. Well, it made sense to get surprised if you heard your friend described as a monster. Yet the man looked like he still had some understanding of why the kid would assume it.

"What the hell is up with that guy?" Richard finally asked as he looked over at Jacob.

Jacob seemed to finally have decided to stand his ground. He had heard what the kid said. He knew his friend was out there, and he was a genuine threat from the sound of it. He was his group's strongest bargaining chip along with Caroline. And while Richard didn't have a high opinion of Jacob, he did strike him as a good businessman, one who knew he had just gained another card in his hand.

"He is my friend and coworker, like I told you, and he is particularly good with a bow. And when it comes to fighting, or 'hunting' as he calls it, he gets a bit in the zone per se. He is weird, he is a loner. I quite honestly don't understand much about him, but the one thing I do know is that he's my friend."

Richard looked at Jacob and saw no indication of the man lying about anything.

Whatever he is, Richard thought, *he isn't worth it.*

He had lost enough good men for one day.

Chapter 16
A Bit of Hunting

The arrow whistled through the air toward the unaware boar. It penetrated deep into the chest of the beast as it whimpered and walked only a couple of meters before collapsing. The second beast wasn't any luckier, as an arrow hit it first in its snout, followed by another to the eye shortly after, ending its life nearly instantly.

The final overgrown pig managed only to get hit by a single arrow before it finally saw the attacker. Jake stood on a small hill overlooking the clearing. He made a rather unimpressive figure. Brown hair and eyes, a mediocre face, donning a cloak with a color palette between brown and dried blood. Yeah, he could have looked more fashionable.

The boar charged him and, with its head kept low, managed to avoid any fatal hits. However, it helped it little as he dodged the boar just before it hit him and proceeded to stab his dagger into the side of the beast.

Squealing in pain, it tried to hit him with its tusks, only to once more be evaded and have yet another dagger plunged in its throat. It barely managed to gurgle out a few noises before it, too, collapsed.

Jake smiled to himself as he ripped his knives out of the beast, cleaned them on his cloak, and put them back in the two sheathes he had on his belt. He was starting to enjoy having two melee weapons, having kept the one he took from one of Richard's archers.

He even considered getting the dual-wielding skill at some point, but that was for when he got his next skill selection. And speaking of levels, he took a brief look at his notification, noticing none had been gained yet. Then again, it was only the first group of beasts he had killed since burning Nicholas.

> *You have slain [Boar – lvl 5] – Bonus experience earned for killing an enemy above your level. 16 TP earned*
>
> *You have slain [Boar – lvl 6] – Bonus experience earned for killing an enemy above your level. 32 TP earned*
>
> *You have slain [Boar – lvl 8] – Bonus experience earned for killing an enemy above your level. 128 TP earned*

The one thing he did get out of it was confirmation of his temporary theory that each level of the beasts doubled the amount of TP earned. He still severely doubted that it would work like that all the way, as the multiplication would just get silly at some point.

He also took notice of the part about bonus experience. His current level in his class was 7, yet he was counted as at a lower level. The only explanation he could find was that level was based on his race level and not his class level.

It did seem a bit imbalanced working like that, though. For him to kill a beast at his own level was incredibly easy.

Even if one ignored his Bloodline, he believed that even someone as untalented in combat as Jacob could manage a beast with an equal race level as his own. Were humans simply favored by the system?

He had also noticed that the levels of enemies did indeed increase as he moved further and further into the forest. The place was huge, and he looked forward to knowing what was at the center of this whole tutorial area. In the beginning, the tutorial announcement had mentioned beast lords or something, so perhaps those were there.

Not that it mattered at the current time. What mattered now were levels. He felt free for the first time since entering the tutorial, like the entire world was open for him to explore. Well, the entire world currently being this tutorial area.

Jake, however, quickly noticed a problem. The number of beasts in this area was severely lacking. So, to find more, he kept running inward toward the center of the tutorial area. After only half an hour, where all he encountered was a group of low-level badgers, he finally came to a big clearing with a waterhole in the middle.

Around the water, he counted five deer and what looked like a stag. It had a huge crown of antlers and seemed to be teeming with power. The antlers themselves were unnatural, to say the least, literally glowing with dim light that he saw reflected on the surface of the water.

Jake quickly used Identify on it and was pleasantly surprised.

[? – lvl 13]

Higher level than the boar. Even before using Identify, he could feel that it was stronger. And the antlers also made him believe that the beast had some kind of magical ability. Jake himself was only level 7, and he was a bit unsure if trying to take on this particular group was a wise move.

The five other deer around the stag were also all level 8 or 9. He was confident that he could kill a couple of them before they managed to reach him if he used good positioning, but if they did catch up to him... Yeah, he was not going to outrun them. Four legs were better than two and all that.

The boar had also only been level 10, and it took him all his arrows, and that didn't even kill it. While he doubted that the stag was as resilient as the boar despite its higher level, the fact that it likely had magic was enough of a deterrent.

He thus decided to ignore them for now. After another level in his class, his race would also level, granting him quite a bit more power. By then, he could consider giving it a shot, though waiting for his level 10 skill would probably be wiser.

He quickly backed away from the clearing and went on his way to look for other prey. It did not take him long to come upon another group of beasts.

This group consisted of what looked like a mix of giant chickens and ostriches. A type of flightless bird, based on the fact that their wings were way too small and their build way too bulky. From their long legs, he also assumed they could run at quite a high speed.

They had long necks extending up to a tiny head. What made them remind him of chickens was the fact that he could hear them clucking. They did not, however, peck at plants or for insects, but instead at a dead badger.

Are there really only carnivores in this damn place? he thought. It just felt like a kind of fucked-up and unoptimized ecosystem that, quite frankly, made no sense. There were plants and trees everywhere, and yet not a single animal ate them. Or maybe the docile birds did. Damn those weird-ass birds.

He had attempted to shoot one down on several occasions, but whenever he tried, they just dodged the arrow like it was nothing. He could not Identify them, so he had no idea if they were secretly overpowered super-beasts. But whatever they were, they seemed to have no concerns aside from increasing the ambiance in the forest with their chirping.

But back to the ostriches, which he had decided to just call them. He used Identify on them one by one, finding all three to be level 8.

They were good prey. Their necks were incredibly exposed if hard targets, as they moved constantly while eating.

With no hesitation, he raised his bow and fired an arrow, already drawing another before the first one hit. It hit one of the ostriches and penetrated straight through its neck, hitting a tree behind it. The beasts that hadn't been hit raised their heads from the badger they had been pecking at and spotted Jake as another arrow came. The one that had been hit only made gurgling noises as it spasmed on the ground.

Disappointingly, his next arrow missed as the giant birds managed to avoid it. Not really intentionally, though, as they were just shifting their legs to get into a better posture to attack.

As with all other beasts, the ostriches charged over at Jake the second they spotted him. He managed to shoot another arrow, hitting one of them in the chest, only doing insignificant damage based on it barely reacting. They reached him in mere seconds, and he tossed the bow to the side and drew both his daggers.

The ostriches' fighting style revolved around quick pecks with their beaks, reminiscent of a snake trying to bite, and powerful kicks. Without his danger sense, he would have been pecked to death within seconds.

The flaw in the ostriches' fighting style was how exposed their necks were when they snapped forward. With a backhanded blow, he managed to plunge his dagger into the neck of the one he had wounded earlier. This, however, left him open as the other kicked him. He barely managed to raise his other arm to block as the heavy force of the foot hit him.

The impact made him fly several meters through the air, and he felt his shoulder dislocate. He barely managed to get up and roll to the side before the beast was once more upon him.

He had lost both his daggers at this point, as he had dropped the one not currently stuck in an ostrich's neck when he got kicked. He knew where it was due to his sphere, but the beast didn't look like it wanted to give him time to pick it up. It didn't help that it was pretty much standing on it either.

The beast attacked again, and Jake dodged it once more, biting through the pain from his shoulder as his arm hung uselessly to his side. Dodging was easy enough with only one enemy left and his forever-present Bloodline ability. The ostrich finally managed to slip up, as it attempted to peck him but ended up smashing its head into a tree instead.

Jake was once more reminded of the power of the peck when he saw its beak penetrate the tree. The power worked against it this time, as it was unable to pull it out from the tough bark again, leaving it stuck. Jake quickly pulled an arrow from his quiver and stabbed it through the exposed and immobile neck.

The beast struggled for a bit before it, too, finally fell dead from the blood loss. He quickly checked his notification and was disappointed by the lack of any levels.

You have slain [Ostrich – lvl 8] – Bonus experience earned for killing an enemy above your level. 128 TP earned

You have slain [Ostrich – lvl 8] – Bonus experience earned for killing an enemy above your level. 128 TP earned

You have slain [Ostrich – lvl 8] – Bonus experience earned for killing an enemy above your level. 128 TP earned

He was still completely unsure how the hell the system decided on the names of these beasts. Most of them seemed just to be "generic animal," even if they weren't completely equivalent to that animal. Then there was also the big piggie that, for some reason, was called an Irontusk Boar. The tusks weren't even made of iron!

Shaking his head, he once more questioned why he wasted so much time pondering meaningless questions, which in itself was a meaningless question.

Looking at his side, he inspected the shoulder that was clearly dislocated, and while he knew that you could "snap" it into place, it was not something he had ever done or tried. He had seen some videos on the internet of it done, and it seemed easy enough...

What followed was Jake spending a bit over half an hour positioning his arm in weird ways, slamming his shoulder into trees, and doing weird movements trying to snap it back in place. The pain was excruciating, and he cursed himself for not just drinking a healing potion or something.

Deciding to take a break from his self-inflicted torture, he sat down on a stone as his shoulder sent waves of pain throughout his body. While wondering how the hell to fix it, he suddenly felt his arm shift slightly as it snapped into place.

It turned out that his body would heal something like a dislocated shoulder by itself if he just gave it a bit of time. The wonders of Vitality, it seemed. So, spending thirty minutes turned out to just be an incredible act of masochism for no damn reason. He was even pretty sure he saw one of those damn birds throw a condescending glance at him.

Jake once more cursed himself as he collected his things. He picked up the bow he had dropped earlier as well as both daggers. He had to get his annoyance out on something and quickly found another group of ostriches, only two of them this time: one level 8 and one level 9.

This fight, however, went way easier. He picked the level 9 one off right away and managed to injure the level 8 one with two arrows before it even reached him.

Instead of trying to dance around evading it, he baited it into pecking a tree, followed by a quick decapitation with one swift swipe of his knife.

> *You have slain [Ostrich – lvl 9] – Bonus experience earned for killing an enemy above your level. 256 TP earned*
>
> *You have slain [Ostrich – lvl 8] – Bonus experience earned for killing an enemy above your level. 128 TP earned*

*'DING!' Class: [Archer] has reached level 8 –
Stat points allocated, +1 Free Point*

*'DING!' Race: [Human (G)] has reached level
4 – Stat points allocated, +1 Free Point*

This fight netted him the levels he wanted. He briefly considered going back for the stag now but decided against it. The ostriches had reminded him that a beast could easily take you by surprise, and it would be quite stupid to suddenly get insta-killed by some mega magic antler-beam.

He instead proceeded to hunt down more beasts in the area. He mainly found lower-leveled deer and badgers, but any kill was worth it. He got a couple of scratches here and there, the worst being when he engaged a group of four low-level badgers, none above level 4.

It quickly turned out, however, that there were not only four badgers. Instead, another seven were hidden in the nearby bushes, and they all ran at him simultaneously. The following fight turned out to be grueling. He managed to kill three of them before they reached him but had to bring out his daggers for the remaining eight.

None of the newcomers were above level 5, but he took a lot of damage as he cut them down one by one. His Sphere of Perception, in concert with his instincts and danger perception, allowed him to minimize the damage he took, but avoiding all attacks was impossible.

He ended the fight with only 56 health remaining, his cloak once more blood-soaked, now also filled with holes and tears. The worst part was that the whole thing did not even give him a damn level.

And to make a shitty situation even shittier, the entire horde only gave him a measly 62 TP. Most of them had been level 2 and 3, with only one at level 5, making the points given abysmal. He quickly told himself that he would not waste time on beasts too far below his level anymore.

He drank a healing potion, which restored nearly 300 HP and refilled his health pool completely.

Add another question to the list: How much does an inferior-rank healing potion heal?

He sighed as he got up, looking at the carnage around him. Only a couple of hours had passed since he last cleaned himself, and he was now once again covered in blood from head to toe.

While he had to admit he was thoroughly enjoying himself in the forest, he did kind of miss the ability to take a nice warm shower. He would have to bring that up with the manager of the tutorial at an opportune time.

CHAPTER 17
LOOT

Jake considered taking a quick trip to clean off all the blood but decided against it. Chances were, he was going to get dirty again from all the fighting one way or another. He instead picked up his bow, which he had dropped during the fight with the horde of badgers.

He started looking for more prey to hunt. While walking, he also conjured more arrows in order to fill his quiver. He had no idea what he would do if he did not have this magical quiver. He imagined having to make every single arrow manually and shivered at the thought.

While walking, he got an idea that could perhaps help alleviate his issues locating prey. To find something to hunt and get a good view of his surroundings, he found the biggest tree he could. The thing easily exceeded eighty meters and towered over the nearby trees.

The climb itself was surprisingly easy. The stats had made Jake's grip strength strong enough to grab the small imperfections in the rough bark and easily climb. It took him a couple of minutes as he finally got above the tree-line of the surrounding trees and activated his Archer's Eye.

His vision turned sharper, and he looked around him. He could see the spot where they had initially entered the tutorial, and in the distance, he still saw the vast wall. His suspicions that this whole place was a sphere were only fortified, as his now even more improved vision allowed him to see details he couldn't before.

The curvature of the wall in the distance was slight but noticeable. It was bending for sure. Jake could not see the base or top of the wall properly, but if his guess of the spherical design was correct, they would naturally extend to the sky.

After looking a bit more around, he saw something glinting in a tree a couple hundred meters away from him. It was slightly above his eye level and was in another of the super-tall trees, one even more massive than the one he was currently sitting in. He was nearly seventy meters up at this point, and this glinting object was perhaps a hundred meters up.

Despite his Archer's Eye's effectiveness, he could not see what it was, only increasing his curiosity. He decided to climb down the tree and head toward the even taller tree with the shiny object. Who doesn't like shiny things, right?

On the way, he encountered a small group of deer, all level 7, which he easily killed. Once again, he didn't receive a level. The only thing he got out of it was a bit of TP and even more blood on him that he couldn't be bothered to wash off.

He quickly reached the tree and, once more, started climbing. It went easy enough like before. He kept looking at the bark as he rose, searching for what had been reflecting the light.

Finally, he spotted what seemed like a hole in the tree trunk above him. When he got up there, he saw that the opening was more than big enough for him to climb into. The tree was, after all, massive, having a diameter above five meters. When he got into the hole, he finally spotted what had returned the light.

A shining box of either bronze or brass decorated with pretty jewels was sitting on a small wooden platform. The hole was far from big enough for Jake to stand in, but he could still crawl. Before he crawled to the box, he focused on his Sphere of Perception and looked for any potential traps.

Overly paranoid or not, Jake found it rather suspicious for jeweled boxes to be found in giant trees. And yet his suspicions were unfounded as he saw nothing indicating a trap or any foul play. It was just a perfectly normal jeweled box in a perfectly normal tree-hole. He was unable to see what was inside the box even with his sphere, and quickly found the reason as he used Identify on it:

[Magical Jeweled Lockbox (Uncommon)] – A system-created magical lockbox enchanted with the ability to block off all types of attempts to peek inside before opening.

He nearly got the sense that the part about blocking out peepers was directly aimed at him. *Sorry for having an omnipresent perception ability, I guess?*

The box was able to block him out and was apparently created by the system. It was also the first uncommon-rarity item he had encountered since entering the tutorial. It was the highest level of rarity he had seen thus far everywhere; everything else was, at most, common rarity. Well, that was ignoring his Bloodline ability and the translation skill, which did not have any rarity ranking besides just being unique.

His suspicions of the box were lessened, but he was still a bit unsure if it was safe to open. Then again, unless the system was just being a complete dick, he saw no reason for an all-powerful entity to leave a killer box in a tutorial. Though it could be a mimic? Everyone loves mimics, right? *I hope it isn't a mimic.*

While the tutorial had not been benevolent in any way, it did seem to have a sense of fairness. Such as beasts not hunting at night, water being plentiful, and the beasts being edible. The beasts were also all relatively passive, only really attacking if you attacked them first.

Having decided to risk it, he crawled to the box and found it had no lock, despite it being called a lockbox. It had only a small mechanism that you could turn to open. He opened the box, once more cautious as to its contents.

Inside was a pair of leather bracers. They seemed to be made from very high-quality leather, and he quickly identified them.

> [Leather Bracers of the Novice Rogue (Uncommon)] – A pair of bracers made of fine leather, originally designed for new initiates in the Order of Umbra. Enchantments: Self-Repair. +5 Agility, +3 Strength. Increases the effectiveness of all stealth skills, further amplified while remaining hidden in the shadows.
>
> Requirements: Lvl 5+ in any class or humanoid race. Stealth-based skill.

Well, if that isn't something, Jake thought happily reading through the item description. While he had no idea what the Order of Umbra was or whatever, the bonus to the stats and his stealth was more than welcome. Also, the fact that they could apparently self-repair was pretty damn cool.

But the mere fact that such equipment existed hidden in this forest was a huge discovery. So far, Jake had not been looking for things like the lockbox with his Sphere of Perception, which, while passively active at all times, did not really make him notice anything that was not moving unless he was looking for it purposely.

He could have moved past several of such lockboxes already. Or perhaps not. None of the other humans he had encountered so far had any equipment not provided during the introduction, so such lockboxes were likely not just lying around.

Jake picked up the bracers from the lockbox, and as soon as he had them in his hands, the box slowly sank into the wooden platform. He could see that the box was not actually merging into the tree with his sphere; it was just... disappearing. When the final part of the box sank into the wood, all traces of the container having ever existed vanished with it. Very similar to what had happened with the giant pillar at the beginning of the tutorial.

He put on the bracers, finding it relatively easy. The leather was strong, far more robust than any other material he had seen with that kind of flexibility. He could likely even block swords and daggers with them, as their cutting resistance seemed extraordinary.

After fully equipping them, he didn't actually feel any different. He tried fiddling with them a bit, making sure they were strapped correctly and all. As he was beginning to wonder if they were broken or whether he didn't meet the requirements to equip them, he got the idea to inject mana into the bracers as he had done with his quiver.

The response came instantly. Jake felt his mana flow into the bracers completely unimpeded and immediately sensed a warm rush through his body, similar to when he leveled up. He felt the Strength and especially the Agility, as 5 extra stat points were not a minor matter at this stage. It was more stat points total than a level in his class.

Taking out his dagger, he tried cutting the bracers, finding little leeway. What he did find, however, was the small mark he made on the bracers disappeared in only a couple of seconds. That repair function sure seemed handy, as he had absolutely no experience in maintaining any of his gear.

That could also be seen as his daggers having dulled slightly compared to the beginning, but they remained sharp enough to kill beasts. He had a feeling they would soon start to become dull, though.

Finding nothing else interesting in the tree, he climbed down after scouting a bit around, taking advantage of his tall vantage point. Besides the vista being quite beautiful, he also spotted a group of animals that he did not immediately recognize when he was halfway down the tree and decided to make them his next target.

He could have spent some more time experimenting with how exactly the equipment worked with the system, but he was far more interested in testing its effects in combat. He could do stuff like that later. Right now, he was looking for a fight.

After a brief stroll that was faster than his pre-tutorial top sprinting speed, he arrived at the hill where he had seen the beasts. These were... different. They looked like hairless rodents or rats or something. Molerats perhaps? Either way, they were as ugly as sin.

Their frightening appearance was only made worse by their size. The beasts were big. Not dog-size big, but

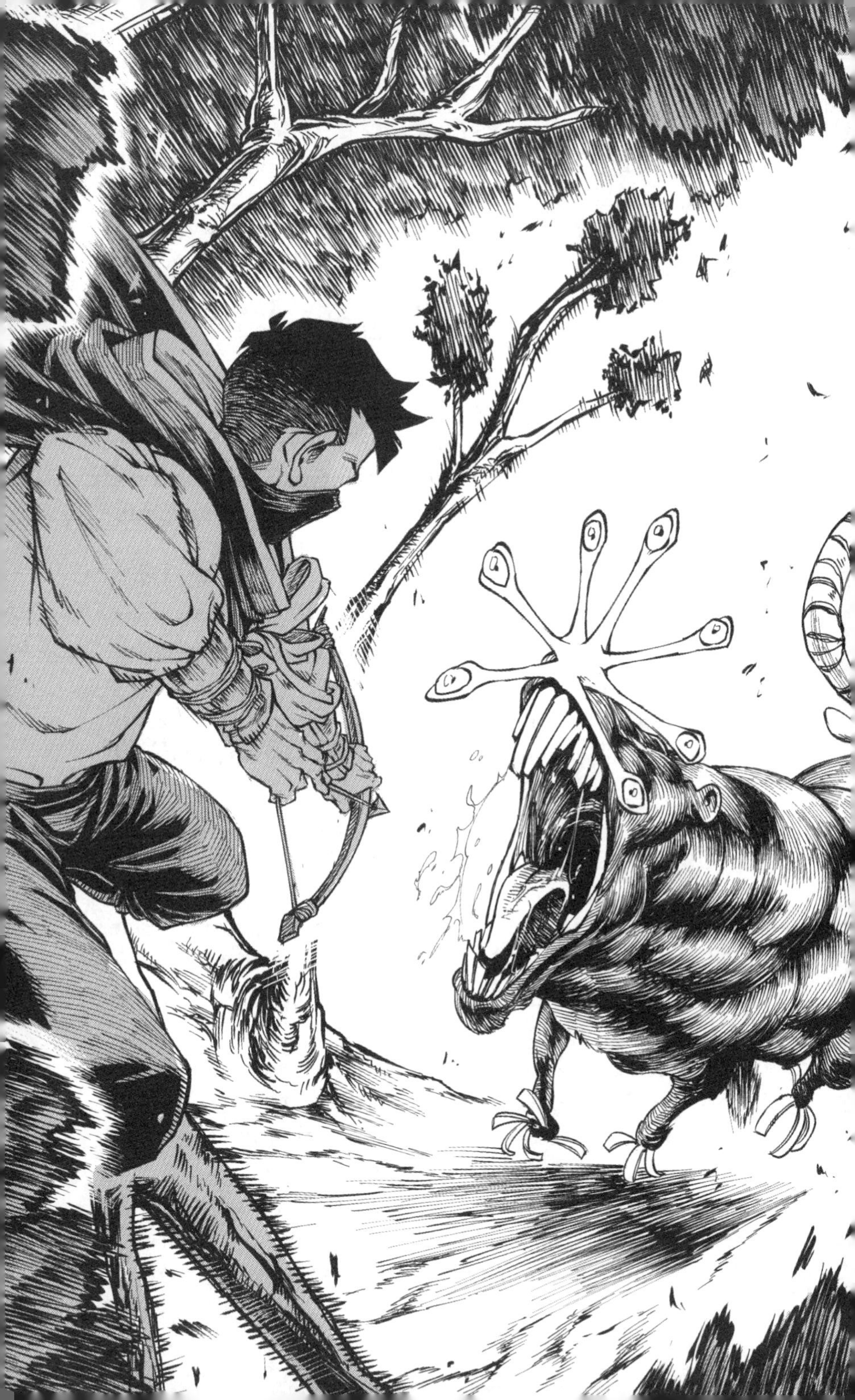

pony-size big. Despite them being on four legs, they were nearly at Jake's eye height. Inspecting them, he was not very surprised.

[??? – lvl 10]
[??? – lvl 10]

There were only two of them, but both were level 10, the same level as the big boar. But he was different than he'd been then. He had leveled plenty, and he even had the new bracers that increased his offensive power significantly.

These rats had weak defenses, according to his initial assessment, which made him confident in facing them. Even if he could not kill both, killing one and then escaping would also be worth it.

But more so than any logical justifications, he just wanted to fight them. A hunt had to not be utterly unbalanced to be interesting, after all.

He decided to get a bit more tactical as he climbed a nearby tree. The two rats were both situated on a hill, just idling about. He could attack them on the hill, but if he decided to run, they would chase him on a downward slope, which seemed like a bad idea for several reasons.

Instead, he would bombard them from a tree and force them to come to him.

After finding a suitable tree, he climbed it and got in position. Chances were they could climb trees, so he decided on a spot where he could also conveniently shoot down the trunk in case they followed up after him.

He nocked an arrow and drew his bow. He lined up his shot and waited for the one closest to him to stop moving. Finding his chance, he released the arrow and saw it fly true, hitting the rat in the side of its head and penetrating all the way into the brain, as he had hit its ear-canal. He was quite proud of that one.

The beast squealed in a noise far louder than anything he had ever heard before. It was loud enough to make his ears ring, and he missed his second arrow due to feeling slightly dizzy. The molerat-thing he'd hit in the brain earlier somehow started rushing toward him with its friend but was unable to properly run, as it kept stumbling and making spasms. It ended up falling over itself and started scratching at the ground.

However, Jake had little time to think as the uninjured molerat still got closer, leaving its squirming friend behind. He managed to get his dizziness under control as he shot another arrow, hitting the now formerly undamaged beast in its back.

The molerat only hissed a bit as it reached the tree, yanked its claws into the wood, and started climbing in small jumps. Jake turned his bow toward it and had a clear shot down the trunk. As the beast was climbing head-first, he managed to hit it in the side of its head.

What followed was another loud squeal; this one, however, was far closer to him. The pain was unbelievable as he lost all hearing, and he felt blood drip out of his ears. All his senses were completely thrown off, and he nearly stumbled and fell down from the tree.

He managed to steady himself, however, as his danger sense kicked in. The beast was just about to bite his leg off when he managed to barely grab a branch above him, lifting his legs. As it prepared to snap at him, he swung back and kicked it square in its ugly mug.

The rat made another squeal as it lost its grip on the tree and fell down. Jake was somehow thankful that his eardrums had already ruptured, since he was unable to hear this squeal. He could still feel the vibrations in the air from it, though, showing just how ridiculous it was.

The beast landed pretty hard on the ground, and the far-too-large rat's problems only got worse as an arrow once more struck it. It tried to get back up and climb the tree again, but Jake kept firing arrows at it every time it tried, making it fall back down time and time again.

After a bit, the beast ran out of strength and collapsed. It was still making small movements but appeared unable to get back up.

He then turned his attention toward the rat he had first shot. He had not yet gotten any kill notifications, so he knew it was still alive.

What he saw was the beast clawing at the ground around it, still trying to make it to him. It walked like it was blackout drunk. Jake guessed he had managed to hit the beast's brain in a pretty important place, yet not somewhere important enough to kill it. He felt a tinge of pity as he fired more arrows at it.

After he had shot a couple, he got a notification from the other one that had finally bled out beneath him. Less than half a minute later, the other one also died.

You have slain [Molerat Screecher – lvl 10] – Bonus experience earned for killing an enemy above your level. 500 TP earned

You have slain [Molerat Screecher – lvl 10] – Bonus experience earned for killing an enemy above your level. 500 TP earned

'DING!' class: [Archer] has reached level 9 – Stat points allocated, +1 Free Point

He breathed out a sigh of relief as he finally got the level. The name of the rats was not surprising and also had more flair than the lower-leveled ones. 500 TP was also not the 512 he would have expected if the double-TP-every-level hypothesis held true, which meant that sadly there would be no level 30 beasts giving millions of TP a kill.

He was now convinced that something happened at level 10 to make the beasts significantly stronger. The huge boar and these rats had been far more powerful than level 9 beasts. Their stats at least were higher by a considerable margin.

Jake sat down on the ground to relax for now, as he allowed his ears time to heal. He at least hoped they would recover. His health points had barely been dented, so drinking a healing potion would be pointless. After only a couple of relaxing minutes, he heard something pop, and sound once again returned to his world.

He smiled at the wonders of Vitality as he climbed down from the tree. There was no time to waste sitting around doing nothing. Time was of the essence and all that. After all, there were more beasts to hunt and, from his recent discovery, loot to be found.

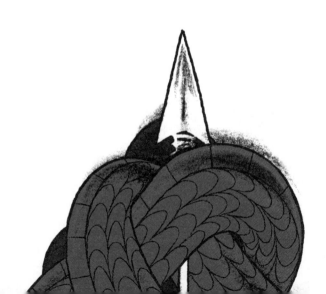

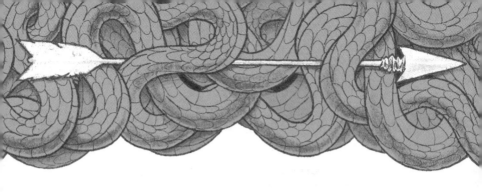

CHAPTER 18
FINDING A CHALLENGE

Jake ripped his knife out of the fallen Irontusk Boar, the same kind he had killed when he was still with his party. The level 10 beast had been quite the challenge for their entire team then, but this time, he took it down solo with little trouble. It still took a bit more than twenty arrows in total, but the beast did fall. It was by far the most resilient beast out there.

Like its brethren, this one had been surrounded by a bunch of small level 1 and 2 boars, all of which were quickly culled during the fight.

The boar was strong, fast, and a boss when it came to taking hits. But all it did was charge back and forth, attempting to trample him. He just had to kite it around and make it smash into things until it died.

However, his reason for attacking this particular boar group was not solely for the sweet experience. The reason was that he had spotted an object in his Sphere of Perception hidden within a hollow log in the middle of the pig's clearing.

In the log was hidden a small box. However, this box was not a nice jeweled one, but just bronze. Identify confirmed it indeed wasn't as good as the jeweled one.

> [Magical Bronze Lockbox (Common)] – A system-created magical lockbox enchanted with the ability to block off all types of attempts to peek inside before opening.

Nevertheless, beggars couldn't be choosers. He opened the lockbox and found a small round object. It looked like a stone coin. Not wasting any more time wondering what exactly he was holding, he identified it.

> [Tutorial Equipment Upgrade Token (Common)] – Upgrade any basic starting item from the tutorial to common rarity.

This item was by far the most game-like he had encountered. Just a straight-up upgrade token. Not that Jake was in any way disappointed by the result. The thought of upgrading his cloak or bow was a welcome one.

He did not even consider upgrading his knife despite how much he used it. After all, his goal was never to use the dagger unless absolutely necessary, and a stronger bow would allow him to kill things easier.

His quiver was also out of the question because it was already common rarity. Quite self-explanatory, really.

It was a tossup between the bow and cloak, then. Looking at this cloak, he saw it was tattered and badly damaged, so Jake wondered what the effect of upgrading it would be. If it mended the thing, it nearly made it worth it.

The bow would likely increase the damage he could do. He had thought that his increased Strength would make the bow less effective by now, as he would draw it fully. He even feared that he would end up snapping it at one point. However, the bow had held up strong, and he had not felt its durability reach any limits quite yet.

In fact, it almost felt like it kept getting more durable along with him. Like it somehow adjusted to his higher stats and kept the string taut and the wood healthy and resilient. It was a bit like some of the more modern compound bows with adjustable draw strength.

Those used technology and physics, though, while Jake's current wooden bow used magic or system-fuckery of some kind. Ultimately, it didn't matter much; what mattered was that his current bow was still capable of fully supporting his fighting style.

Thus, he decided to try and upgrade his cloak. He took it off and laid it across a stone as he held the token up. He was wondering how to use it as a window popped up.

> **Use [Tutorial Equipment Upgrade Token (Common)] on [Archer's Cloak (unranked)]?**

He quickly agreed, and the token turned to dust that was carried off by the wind. At the same moment, his cloak rapidly mended and was cleaned of all the blood and dirt. It was like new again. It didn't look like it had changed much except for a good dry-cleaning in a quick visual inspection.

Touching it, however, it felt far less coarse than before and far more comfortable to wear. Jake quickly focused on it and used Identify.

> **[Archer's Cloak (Common)] – A cloak handed out for the tutorial, now upgraded with a token. Made of resilient cloth that is**

> resistant to slashing attacks. Enchantments:
> Self-Repair.
>
> Requirements: Tutorial Attendee. Archer Class

While certainly less impressive than his bracers, the Self-Repair enchantment itself made it worth it. Finally, he would not walk around looking like a murderhobo. Well, he kind of still looked like a murderhobo, just one wearing a nice cloak.

He felt quite a bit better now that he didn't have the constant smell of sweat and blood enter his nostrils at every moment. He proceeded to scout a bit around, looking for more lockboxes. Finding nothing, he noticed it starting to get a little darker. He opened the tutorial panel to see what the time said.

> **Tutorial Panel**
> Duration: 62 days & 15:22:58
> Total Survivors Remaining: 965/1200
> TP Collected: 7335

It had been around noon when they entered this place. With the timer saying fifteen hours now, that meant it had to be around 6 pm or so?

He thought about what his plans for the night would be. He did not feel tired in the least as of yet, probably due to his improved stats. He also took small breaks between battles. While the physical exertion did matter, mental exhaustion was the real killer. He had to stay sharp.

Hunting in the night was certainly an option, but he had no idea how the beasts would react. They seemed not to be very active, but he doubted they would just leave him alone if he started to attack them. The problem, however, would be finding them hidden in the shade of the trees.

His Sphere of Perception offered him a great way of scouting his immediate surroundings, but it provided no way of seeing far ahead.

But then he thought of some caves he had seen earlier when he looked for loot. His sphere would be incredibly useful in a small, closed-off space. And it would be completely dark—something mattering little to him with his sphere, but would likely handicap the beasts living in there somewhat.

He did realize that caves were not the ideal place to fight for a ranged combatant like him, but he decided to give it a shot anyway. Besides, what place would be better to hide lockboxes than caves?

But before then, he still had daylight to burn, beasts to hunt, and loot to... well, loot.

He spent the next couple of hours looking for boxes and killing beasts, but quickly noticed the issue of finding high-level beasts. He still had the stag to go back for, but the beast continued to give him a distinct sense of danger.

He tried to ignore anything below level 8, but still killed a couple. Then he noticed a huge issue: humans.

Several groups were still walking the forest. Jake avoided them like the plague, but that did result in him missing out on several beasts to kill. He wasn't going to attack other humans either. While Jake had killed quite a handful already, all of them had been in self-defense. Alright, so he had baited some of them to attack him, but it was still *kinda* self-defense.

Either way, he wasn't going to go full psycho and begin hunting people. So he stayed hidden.

By the time the moon was out, and it was starting to get really dark, he had barely killed anything, gotten no levels, and found no lockboxes.

The only positive aspect was that his new cloak turned out to be great, especially when he combined it with his new bracers. They were incredibly strong, and he even had a level 9 badger bite down on them, discovering that its teeth were unable to pierce all the way through.

The cloak also got some tears and a few small holes during his hunt, but they repaired themselves quickly.

He was currently sitting on a root and leaning against a tree as he conjured more arrows. It started to get too dark to hunt properly, and the beasts had also begun going idle. He had seen a group of deer that all seemed to be sleeping.

He decided to finally head to one of the caves he had seen embedded in a hill earlier, with it being too late to hunt anymore. Or perhaps calling it a hole in a hill would be accurate, as it did not actually consist of rock.

He got to the cave—which, yes, he had decided to call it a cave anyway—and looked inside. It seemed rather unassuming, like most of the other caves he had encountered, but this one gave him a bit of a special feeling. He couldn't quite put his finger on why, but he felt like there was something special about it.

Walking inside, he quickly found himself in complete darkness after barely entering and taking a single turn. The hill hadn't been that big from the outside, but the path was sloping downward.

As he walked, he found no beasts or enemies of any kind. All he saw was a musty cave. As he got further and further in, he spotted faint light in the distance. His sphere instantly made him aware that the source of light was small fungi.

Getting closer to them, he saw they were glowing blue mushrooms. Intrigued, he tried using Identify, only to be met with a generic [Mushroom] message. Yeah, he was going to avoid touching those as he walked in further.

He quickly noticed that he was walking in a circle, with the downward pattern continuing like a spiral staircase. The mushrooms only became more numerous as he descended, soon not only being on the ground but also the walls and the ceiling.

When dark green moss also started appearing on the wall, he considered going back. He was not very educated when it came to fungi, but he knew that they could be dangerous even if he didn't touch them.

And he currently found himself in a small, closed-off space surrounded by them, with potentially deadly spores floating in the air all around him. His Sphere of Perception was quite overpowered, but it did not allow him to spot minuscule objects like spores or particles of dust.

Fungi liked to grow in damp places. The cave certainly fit that criteria, but so did human lungs. The fact that a fungus could take root inside the body was precisely why they could be so dangerous.

He remembered some friends of his family who'd had a bad case of mold in their house, and they'd only found out when their youngest kid got really sick. It was an invisible, silent killer.

And these were glowing magic mushrooms. Even if they were just normal ones, if they managed to infect him and take root within his body, would healing potions even do anything? Would his Vitality simply accelerate their growth?

But on the other hand, this place was unique. And if Jake had learned anything from videogames or novels, it was that unique and interesting places contain something equally unique and interesting. That, or it was a bad game.

No risk, no reward, he thought to himself as he kept walking.

More and more moss and mushrooms were growing on the walls as he got further in, and by now, he could not avoid stepping on mushrooms as he walked. Small spores were swept up, visible in the blue light, as he touched the mushrooms.

He covered his mouth with the upper part of his cloak, trying to minimize his intake of air as much as possible. His danger sense was silent, but then again, he had no idea if it worked on passive threats like this. Assuming it was even a threat.

After another ten minutes, he had descended quite a bit, and the mushrooms were at peak growth. The moss had also gotten so bad that it hung from the ceiling.

Turning back now would be too late if these things were infectious anyway, so he decided just to keep walking, hoping to find something worth his time.

After walking for over an hour, he started to regret ever going to this place. Nothing had changed for the entire hour; it was just more of the same. He even guessed he was stuck in a loop or something and tried stabbing an arrow into the dirt wall to serve as a marker.

After walking for another half an hour after that, he had still not encountered his arrow. If he wasn't walking in a circle, exactly how far had he gone? He had to be hundreds of meters down by now.

The only positive aspect was that something good just *had* to be down here. Either that or the system was a massive troll.

A quarter of an hour later, he finally reached the end of the tunnel. What met him was not a dirt wall, however, but a wooden door. The door looked rotten, like it had been here since ancient times, with no apparent door handle.

Looking at his Sphere of Perception, he saw nothing behind the door, making him wonder if this was even a door or just a door-shaped wooden wall. Was it some kind of big wooden shield, maybe? He tried to use Identify on it but got nothing.

Getting nothing from any of his usual means, he did what any reasonable person would do in his situation. He poked it.

Tutorial Challenge Dungeon Discovered!

Challenge Dungeons found throughout the multiverse offer danger and rewards hand in hand, being known as natural treasures. This variant is only found within the Tutorials provided by the system to newly integrated races. Enter at your own risk.

Requirements to enter: Must be below level 10 in any class or race. Must not have a profession. Must be top 5% in tutorial points. Requirements to enter met.

WARNING: Challenge Dungeons cannot be entered in groups. Only 1 challenger allowed per dungeon.

Enter the dungeon?
Y/N

I found something for sure, he thought.

Earlier, he'd thought that lockboxes with loot in them were the most game-like element he had discovered so far, but this was literally a dungeon. Okay, maybe the whole stat thing was also very game-like, but seriously, *dungeons*.

It was well hidden, and he had no doubt it would be dangerous. The requirements to even enter were also quite something. As it required one not to have a profession, did this mean it was related to unlocking one? Or did it have something to do with how strong he was allowed to be?

The last tutorial points were also interesting, as it confirmed him to be in the top 5%. With less than a thousand people alive, that put him in the top fifty. He wasn't sure if he should be happy about it, though, as he knew the only reason for that was killing humans.

Not entering the dungeon did not even occur to him. The thing he desired the most was a good challenge. And this dungeon literally had *"challenge"* in the name. How could he say no?

He checked his equipment, making sure that everything was as it should be. His stamina was still high, and he did not feel even a whiff of fatigue.

He didn't hesitate any longer, and accepted the challenge with great excitement.

The ninety-third universe had been integrated. The enlightened natives had entered their tutorials as the multiverse's forces moved to capitalize on the great shift, to capitalize on the natives and even the tutorials themselves.

For a new universe to be integrated was not only a monumental event for the universe in question, but the entire multiverse. It brought not just expansion but change.

Powerful entities moved to take advantage of the changes. Paths had been opened to even the mightiest of beings. It was an excellent opportunity to break through their limits or further expand their influence.

Others were fearful of the change. Feared what it would bring. These did all they could to solidify their positions.

But some... Some did nothing.

An entity lay in its realm of desolation as it was stirred awake by the great shift. Its eyes opened and stared into the void.

"The ninety-third era has begun, huh," it muttered listlessly before closing its eyes once more—the significant expansion and change of little interest to this being.

Yet it couldn't help but hope that this time something would change. A hope it quickly quelled from its mind as it entered meditation once more.

CHAPTER 19
EVERYBODY LOVES BLUE MUSHROOMS

Challenge Dungeon Entered!

Objective: Survive to the end of the dungeon while accomplishing all challenges presented along the way. Failure to complete challenges may result in death.

Jake felt his vision shift as he blacked out for a brief moment. When he opened his eyes again, he found himself standing in a giant hall. Looking around him, he saw only shattered stones and broken pillars littering the ground, all of it the same monotone gray color. The only slightly different thing was the braziers hanging from the ceiling, emitting a faint blue light.

To his horror, the braziers emitted light not through magic or fire, but by being stuffed with glowing blue mushrooms, the same kind as in the cave. It seemed like even in deadly Challenge Dungeons, one could not escape the power of fungi.

He also noticed that his bow, daggers, and quiver were all mysteriously gone, and checking his satchel, so were all his potions. He really hoped the system would give those back...

Shifting his attention back to the hall, he began looking for where to go. The only entrance or exit was through an opening that looked like it once held a door. Walking through it, he entered a long hallway. It was filled with the same blue light, emitted from even more mushrooms, but this time growing on the walls. Not exactly an improvement.

After walking through the hall, he found himself in yet another one, nearly identical to the entryway he had arrived in. This hall was a bit cleaner, a bit less broken, and even a few cracked pillars were still standing. When he casually strolled into the room, his danger sense exploded. He swiftly retreated into the hallway he had just entered from.

A long metal spike penetrated the floor where he had just been standing, piercing the solid stone like it was butter. To make it worse, Jake then heard a sizzling sound as he saw the ground slowly being eroded. Stupidly, he decided to walk forward and get a closer look.

Before he could examine it properly, another spike came flying straight at him. Like the first, this one was also easily dodged. Jake didn't consciously need to avoid attacks like this; he simply had to follow his instincts. At least that was how he justified moronically walking back into a room he knew wanted to kill him.

Triggering the second spike wasn't completely useless, though. He had noticed it came out of a small hole in the wall, one that disappeared right after firing. He did a few more tests and noted down where in the wall the spikes had come from.

After a bit longer, Jake felt confident enough to make a run toward the hall's exit. Sprinting forth, he quickly dodged the three spikes that were fired after him. A few seconds later, the second barrage came, and he avoided these just as easily.

As he moved in between two pillars that marked the hall's midway point, they both fired spikes at him simultaneously. Jake was surprised and forced to throw himself on the ground before they hit him, barely managing to roll away as another spike came from one of the walls.

What the fuck is this supposed to be? he yelled in his head as he scrambled back on his feet. Luckily, the two pillars didn't shoot again, giving him ample time to keep going.

With no time to waste, he kept running as he closed in on yet another two pillars just in front of the exit. To his slight annoyance, these two didn't do a thing as he safely ran past them, finally leaving the spiky hall behind, only to find himself in another mushroom-filled hallway.

Nothing was happening in the hallway as Jake breathed out in relief, the blue mushrooms now slightly less sore on the eyes. Without his Bloodline, the very first hallway would have likely killed him, or at least maimed him badly. Was this place just some bullshit deathtrap?

A single scratch from those spikes was enough to erode the stone floor, and as he looked back into the hall, he saw smoke rising from where the spikes had hit. Whatever was on those things would likely eat through him in seconds.

As he got up and walked to the end of the hallway, he was met by another system message.

> **Dungeon Challenge: Collect at least four silver mushrooms in the next room.**
>
> **0/10 silver mushrooms collected**

What the hell is up with this dungeon and mushrooms? he grumbled to himself. At least these were silver mushrooms. That must be an improvement, right?

Standing at the opening to the challenge room, he inspected it thoroughly. He saw small pedestals scattered across the hall, each pedestal holding a single silver mushroom. He could currently only see seven pedestals, but he assumed there to be ten in total based on the system message. The rest were obscured by pillars.

He felt like the system was taunting him by only requiring four mushrooms. He would, of course, try to collect all ten. There had to be some kind of extra reward or bonus tied to not just doing the bare minimum. Also, it just seemed more fun that way.

This hall had the same design as the last two. But everything was in even better condition, with the pillars barely having a few cracks. The pedestals also added a lot of flavor to the room. Moving into the hall for only a brief moment, he confirmed that this hall also fired spikes at people. Very rude.

After planning his approach carefully, a very detailed plan appeared in his mind. A plan that could roughly be boiled down to "just wing it." Entering the hall after getting a running start, his sphere informed him that the wall behind him closed itself off when he was five meters into the hall, leaving only a single exit in the distance.

He dashed toward the first silver mushroom and was met with a few spikes heading toward him, as expected. It took little effort to avoid them with his high Perception and Agility, as he approached the pedestal with caution. He kind of expected another trap, but was pleasantly surprised when nothing terrible happened.

> **1/10 silver mushrooms collected**

One down, he thought as he threw the mushroom into his satchel and sprinted toward the next one. Another spike was fired toward him after taking only a few steps, followed by another shortly after.

After having collected four mushrooms, he confirmed that the frequency of spikes was increasing with every mushroom acquired.

He danced across the hall while attempting to stay as far away from the walls and pillars as possible. There were several dangerous situations, one particular event standing out where he nearly got hit by three spikes fired at once. One of them had come from a particularly tricky angle.

He barely avoided getting hit during the final sprint as he rolled over the tenth pedestal, using it for cover and collecting the last mushroom in one fluid motion. The spikes were coming rapidly by now, and without his current stats and Bloodline ability, he doubted that he would have been able to gather all ten without dying.

With all the mushrooms in hand, he made a mad dash toward the exit, practically rolling into the next hallway. This one was, to his surprise, *also* covered in blue mushrooms.

Checking his satchel, he found the expected eight mushrooms, the last two still held in his hands as he placed them into it. The system then once again made its appearance by informing him of his completed task.

> **Dungeon Challenge: Collect at least four silver mushrooms in the next room.**
>
> **10/10 silver mushrooms collected**
>
> **Challenge completed!**

He had kind of hoped for a reward or something for collecting all ten mushrooms. He looked at said mushrooms and used Identify, only to be met with the generic [Mushroom] message. The skill frankly did more harm than good at times.

He proceeded through the hallway, and as he got to the end, he half-expected another challenge room like the others. He was instead met with a new kind of hall, if it could even be called that.

This hall was rather weird. The walls and ceiling looked the same as all the others, and everything was the same bland color palette, but that was where the similarities ended. The pillars were now gone, and nearly the entire floor space was replaced with a huge basin of water, extending from wall to wall.

The only parts of the floor not underwater were several platforms and the beginning of the hall itself.

Exiting the hallway would make him step onto a small ledge just in front of the many platforms. On it were growing even more of those damn mushrooms. The hall itself was also significantly smaller compared to the other ones.

The platforms positioned in the water were small and circular, looking kind of like giant water lilies. They were around a meter and a half in diameter, enough for one person to stand on, but not much more. From where he stood, he saw a glowing blue symbol of sorts on each of them.

As he fully entered the room by stepping out of the hallway, a system message appeared.

> **Dungeon Challenge: Make it to the other side of the hall by using the platforms. The time limit per hall is set to 15 minutes.**
>
> **Make it to the other side of the hall: 0/3**
> **Time remaining: 14:59**

But just as he thought *"that doesn't seem so hard,"* he was met with a follow-up message.

> **All stats reduced to a static 10. All skills are disabled. Stats and skills will be restored upon completion of the challenge**

He instantly felt a wave of weakness wash over him as he knelt down on the floor. His senses dulled from sudden vertigo. He felt sick to his stomach and a need to throw up. It was like he had just gotten done running four marathons while lifting weights on an empty stomach.

Soon after, the feeling went away just as quickly as it had come. But the weakness remained. Jake tried using Archer's Eye and found it unresponsive.

It felt weird to lose his skills; in fact, everything felt off. It was like he had returned to before the system and the tutorial. Well, except for the tiny detail that he was stuck in a room that was likely going to kill him in fifteen minutes if he didn't make his way through it.

Having reduced stats, of course, made the entire challenge quite a bit more complicated. But that didn't mean Jake had time to waste as he began analyzing the room. Using his Sphere of Perception, he saw tha—

Wait, what?

Blinking in confusion, he felt that his Bloodline ability was still active. It hadn't even weakened or been affected in any way. Why did it still work? Was it not considered a skill? But even if it was not, he knew that Perception increased its potency, and yet with his Perception reduced to only 10, it worked like if he still had underfed stats.

It was a mystery that he had no answer to, but a pleasant surprise nonetheless. What exactly was a Bloodline ability? Why did he have one while others seemingly didn't?

Focus, Jake, focus, he admonished himself as he forcefully dismissed the thoughts. He had more important things to deal with than pondering on Bloodlines, such as how not to die. Walking to the edge, he began inspecting the platforms and the symbols engraved on them.

The symbols were intricately made depictions of different animals. Jake saw three different types, the first one a coiled-up snake with a... With a damn mushroom in its mouth.

Suppressing his desire to yell profanities, he inspected the second type. It was another snake-like creature, but this one had wings and spikes growing all over its body—a winged serpent of sorts. The serpent was flying above a myriad of other creatures. He saw both different animals but also human-like depictions.

These animals and humanoid creatures were kneeling or prostrated on the ground, looking up toward the serpent in either worship or fear. Some of them held weapons and looked to be doing rituals, while others simply prayed.

The third and final engraving was what he identified as a wyvern. It had small hands attached to its wings and, like the winged serpent, had spikes growing out of its spine. It looked murderous, to say the least. This wyvern was on a mountain, roaring toward the sky. Like it was angry at the heavens above.

Was this a depiction of the growth cycle for the small snake? Did it evolve from a snake to a wyvern? He had assumed that evolution was a used trope by the system, seeing as he had a race, and said race could level up. The big (G) in front of [Human] was also a huge indicator. But it was still quite something if a small snake could turn into a wyvern.

He had an intuition he was spot on, but the problem was still what the hell he was supposed to do with these platforms and engravings. His only way to the other side of the room was by jumping from platform to platform. He had no desire to enter the water, which he had a suspicion was not even water, based on the clearly poisoned or acid-drenched spikes from the last couple of halls.

After looking around a bit more, it struck him how the blue glow on each platform reminded him of the light given off by the mushrooms. Said mushrooms were growing around where he stood on the ledge, the only other kind of object present. As he looked at the first symbol's picture with the snake eating a mushroom, he got an idea.

He covered his hand with some cloth from his cloak as he picked up one of the mushrooms. He was still a little afraid that the things were poisonous to touch with his bare hands—a fear that would be especially bad to put to the test with lowered stats. He went back to the edge of the ledge with mushrooms in hand and threw one of the mushrooms on a platform depicting a small snake.

The instant the mushroom made contact, it was absorbed into the platform, and the blue glow disappeared. Waiting a bit to see if anything more would happen, the blue light returned after only ten or so seconds.

He tried the same with the other two kinds of platforms but was met with no response. The mushrooms were absorbed, but nothing more happened. Jake tested throwing mushrooms at different platforms for a bit and built up the courage to finally touch the blue buggers without any protection. It didn't seem to poison him, so maybe the things weren't that bad after all?

With his testing done and time ticking down, he had reached a conclusion. After a mushroom hit a platform with a mushroom-eating snake on it, the blue light would disappear for ten seconds, and throwing a mushroom on an already-deactivated platform would refresh the countdown.

Noting down the platforms' positions, he saw several with mushroom-snakes on them between him and the hall's end. The room was well lit, and he could see the depiction of all the different symbols on all the pillars quite clearly. After observing for a while, it clicked for him.

This was clearly a maze. Jake designated the glowing platforms as kill-zones and the non-glowing ones as safe. So he needed a path where he only had to jump between secure platforms. And such a path existed where the only pattern he had to go on was the snake platforms. He was rather confident in his deduction, and he could quite honestly not afford to stall any longer as he looked at the timer.

> **Time remaining: 3:24**

He started plucking mushrooms, putting a bunch in his satchel and holding a couple in each hand. He threw a mushroom on the first platform and saw the light disappear. *Please don't kill me*, he pleaded internally as he jumped.

He landed safely on the platform, and nothing happened. He briefly thanked the clearly evil, yet slightly benevolent mushroom god as he threw another and jumped to that platform as its light disappeared too.

After repeating the same for the following platforms, he finally made it to the other side. He looked at the timer and rushed through the hall's exit to find himself in another nearly identical one. The system appeared again.

> **Make it to the other side of the hall: 1/3**

> **Time remaining: 14:59**

This room also had the mushrooms on the starting platform and a newly added pedestal with a beautiful red silk pillow placed on it. Lying on the pillow was what looked like a dagger. He quickly tried to use Identify on it but was met with no response.

Shit, he thought, having briefly forgotten that skills were disabled. The dagger was made from what looked like bone. Ornate markings depicting a snake decorated its handle, giving Jake a very culty vibe.

He picked up the dagger, momentarily afraid to be cursed or something, but was luckily met with nothing. Scouting out the room, he quickly concluded that no path with only mushroom-eating snake symbols existed, meaning he couldn't repeat the same tactic.

He nevertheless picked up some more mushrooms and also tested throwing one on a snake platform, confirming it to be disabled for ten seconds just like in the previous room. The other platforms also ignored the mushrooms like before. The size of the room and layout were also nearly identical. Indeed, the only difference was the pattern of the symbols and the dagger.

As the counter steadily counted down, his mind worked on overdrive to figure out the solution.

CHAPTER 20
DEATH & COURAGE

As the timer ticked down, he assessed the situation. He knew what to do about the snake platforms, and as he had been given a dagger, he assumed it would have something to do with deactivating either the winged serpent or the wyvern symbols.

If his whole evolution theory was correct, he likely had to do something with the winged serpent symbol. The picture was the same as in the room prior, depicting a winged serpent flying over humanoids and animals, all of whom submitted before the beast.

If he had to feed the mushroom-eating snake mushrooms, did he have to feed the winged serpent too? It seemed probable. There was just one tiny issue. The only other thing than itself in the picture was other living things. And he was the only human or animal present; he didn't like where his logic was going.

But he would have to figure something out. The knife was clearly there to cut something, and the only things he had to cut were stones, mushrooms, and himself. And as much as he would like to go on a rampage slicing and dicing mushrooms, he was pretty sure what to cut. *Well, nothing ventured, nothing gained.*

He lifted the knife and made a small cut in the palm of his hand.

He hissed in pain as it started bleeding. Standing at the edge of the platform, he threw out a few drops of blood, luckily hitting one of the symbols with a winged serpent on it. When the blood touched it, the blue light disappeared, just like it had when he fed the small snake mushrooms.

Smiling to himself, he nodded at his brilliance. *Not that hard.* He started looking for the pattern he would have to jump as he wrapped up his hand in the cloth of his robe. This room's path was a bit longer than the last one, but it should be manageable. *Alright, so first there... then there...*

The seconds ticked by as he mapped out the route in his mind. But he soon noticed an issue. Not with his intended path, but his hand. It hadn't stopped bleeding; in fact, it felt like it was getting worse.

"Fuck me," he cursed out loud, as he'd just put himself on an even tighter timer.

He quickly went for the pattern he had decided on and started throwing mushrooms and blood all around him as he leaped on the first platform. It made his bleeding hand hurt as it was unwrapped from his cloak, but quite frankly, he wasn't sure it could get any worse.

As he got a bit over halfway, he started feeling dizzy and nearly stumbled. The blood was coming out at a frightening speed, and his attempts to put pressure on the wound didn't do jack shit.

He kept pushing forward as his hand began to feel cold, a coldness that soon spread up his arm. A sense of weakness began to overtake his entire body as he finally made it to the last platform and, with a half-hearted leap, tried to jump into the next hallway.

His half-heartedness resulted in him not getting all the way, hitting the ledge hard. He managed to hang on with his barely functional arms, but his feet ended up barely touching the water.

The moment they made contact, he felt a stinging pain. He hauled himself up with a rush of adrenaline, but as he tried to stand up, he heard a weird sound that resembled someone squashing rotten fruit.

When he fell on the ground, the feelings of pain and dizziness were overpowering. He looked behind him and saw the fate of his feet. Both were rotting stumps as blackness spread up his legs, already up to his thighs.

He tried crawling forward, but his knees gave in, as even the bone was rotten. He was so close to being all the way into the hallway.

With desperation, he used his hands to claw himself forward. His entire body was cold, but the debilitating pain from his legs made him focus. Even then, his vision started to blur as he kept crawling. Vision in his left eye suddenly gave out, followed by the right eye. He was blinded. The rot had spread to his lower body by now, already reaching the navel.

His mind was blank, yet he kept clawing at the ground, moving him forward inch by inch. It wasn't even clear if one could call him conscious any longer. His instinct to survive was the only thing still hanging on. The rot had already reached parts of his lungs, and breathing became impossible. Soon it would reach his heart, and no matter how powerful his instinct to survive, that would be the end.

As death was mere moments away, he crawled the last few centimeters, fully entering the hallway.

> **Challenger fully restored. Challenge continuing.**
>
> **Make it to the other side of the hall: 2/3**
>
> **Time remaining: 14:59**

Jake opened his eyes with a jolt as all feeling returned to his body. He was already standing up before he could process what had happened. His body was healed, the knife wound and rot all gone, and even his clothes restored.

His heart was still pumping fast, and his entire body stiff. It took him around a minute before he finally calmed down, fully realizing what had just happened. Realizing that he was no longer in danger.

He had more or less died. He'd felt himself die. While the feeling of coldness and emptiness was physically gone, it still dominated his mind. For the first time since he'd entered the tutorial, he had truly faced death. His Bloodline ability had offered no warning, and he'd had no response to his body being slowly devoured.

If the system had not healed him when it did, he would be dead. There was nothing he could do about it. He enjoyed fighting. He enjoyed dancing between life and death, dodging fatal attacks by the skin of his teeth. To feel the rush from coming out on top.

But against that water, or whatever that liquid was... It wasn't really an enemy. It was just there. If he died fighting a strong opponent, even if it was a mindless beast with no ability to comprehend his sentiment, he could accept it.

Dying here alone, his only companions being mushrooms... He couldn't accept such a fate. He wanted to die fighting, not lying on the ground helplessly, slowly being corroded by some shitty toxic dungeon water.

On that note, what the fuck was up with this shitty dungeon? Weren't dungeons supposed to be loot-filled caves with strong enemies and cool bosses? Not just a bunch of sucky halls with even suckier traps? Was this one of those puzzle-dungeons nobody likes in videogames? Could one even call this shithole a dungeon to begin with?

His despair and concern turned to anger as he shifted his attention back to the present. He had lived, he was alive, and he wasn't going to die in this fucking place. With newfound resolve, he proceeded into the final hall.

On the way, he picked up the bone dagger that had been placed in the hallway with him. He had dropped it during the last challenge, but it appeared that the system wanted him to have it still.

If the next challenge was like the others, he would perhaps have to cut his hand once more. This time, however, he swore to make the wound smaller and to not dilly-dally before beginning. Also, to not be a freaking moron and cut his palm. Why was that even a thing? The palm had many nerves in it, and it had to be moved all the time, making it hurt even more.

The next hall was yet again pretty much the same. Except for the pedestal with the dagger and the pattern of symbols, nothing had changed. But as he looked at the design of the platforms, he was taken aback.

There was no longer a maze. Instead, all of the platforms were neatly organized in rows, meaning one could take the entire trip while only stepping on a single type. Did this mean that one could just throw a couple of mushrooms and go the easy snake route?

No, that felt wrong. Jake tried to throw a mushroom on the snake platform, and it indeed did turn off for ten seconds just like all the others. Was this a free room? A mind game? A trap?

He looked at the rows and noticed that only the middle one solely consisted of the wyvern symbols. The wyvern was sitting on a mountaintop, roaring toward the sky. There was nothing else shown in the picture.

The others he'd had to feed something, giving them what they wanted. But what did this wyvern want? There were only two objects on the entire image: the wyvern and the mountain. He doubted a bit of blood or a mushroom or two would satisfy it.

The only clue he could see was it staring toward the heavens as it roared. Was it angry at the sky? But that led to the question... Why was it just sitting on the mountain? The wings were open as if it wanted to take flight.

A thought suddenly entered his mind. He wasn't sure if it was his own intuition or maybe even the dungeon itself implanting that thought. But somehow, he felt like the wyvern looked... hesitant. He wasn't sure if "afraid" would be a better word, but something within the wyvern held it back. The roar was not one of anger or indignation, but one of doubt.

It was only a feeling, but his intuition told him he was right. At least partly. What the wyvern truly needed was courage. The willpower to advance and face its fears. As he thought this, the platforms appeared to respond as their glow increased.

At the same time, every other platform but the ones with wyverns on turned off. Jake instinctively knew he could move down any of the different paths toward the exit and move on safely. But he didn't.

Instead, Jake decided to feed the wyvern courage. Without hesitation, he sprinted toward the still glowing platforms with the blue symbols of the wyvern. He leaped onto the first platform, and his danger sense instantly went insane.

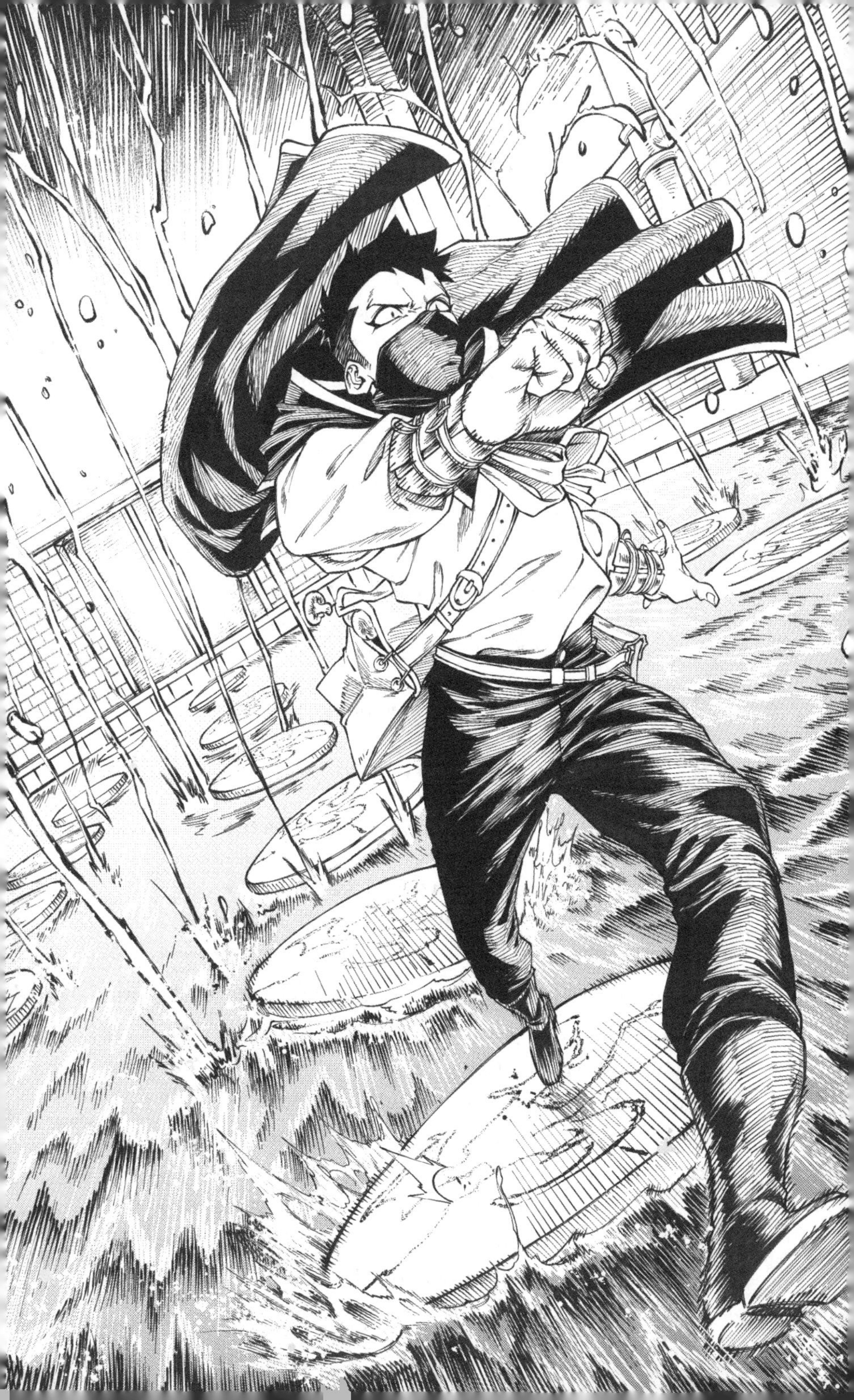

He didn't stop for even half a second as he jumped onto the next platform with a wyvern on it. Through his sphere, he felt the platform behind him being consumed by a torrent of the acidic water shooting up.

He repeatedly jumped, leaping from one platform to another until he reached the end, every platform behind him consumed by the water.

As he stood there, the challenge passed, he looked back and saw all the other platforms crumble to dust. He turned to the doorway and proceeded out of the hall, leaving the entire room behind him in shambles.

> **Dungeon Challenge: Make it to the other side of the hall by using the platforms. The time limit per hall is set to 15 minutes.**
>
> **Make it to the other side of the hall: 3/3**
>
> **Challenge passed!**
>
> **Hidden challenge completed: Show the courage to do what's necessary. Hidden bonus room unlocked.**
> **All Stats restored. All skills are reactivated.**

A wonderful feeling went through his body as all of his stats returned. It only lasted a few moments as everything returned to normal. He was amazed that he did not need to adapt to his body being strengthened so drastically.

But then again, it was only him returning to the same strength he'd had around... shit, only half an hour ago.

As he read through the message, he also realized that he could indeed just have taken the easy path. If his guess was correct, then the previous room had been a test to see if the challenger would take the obvious and easy route, or take a risk like he had.

He smiled to himself at his foolhardiness. Well, he thought, at least I would have died on my own terms if it failed.

Entering the next room, the one he assumed to be a bonus one, he found himself in *yet another* hall. This one was far bigger, though, so that was something. There were no pillars like the first or a massive basin of killer-water like the subsequent ones. It was just a long hall with a gigantic mural carved into the wall at the end.

He walked closer, and as he did so, he could finally see the whole carving. It clearly told a story. As he stared, the images began to move and suck his consciousness into them. The moving pictures displayed the same snake from the symbols as it crawled on the ground, eating mushrooms.

It only continued for a few moments as the snake consumed mushroom after mushroom. The same tiny snake soon began fighting giant beasts, but they were all left half-rotten in its wake. The little snake slowly grew in size, before it finally grew wings and soared into the sky.

It flew over the landscape, spitting out a mist that consumed the very land beneath it. At other times, humanoid beings of different shapes were shown kneeling before the great serpent as it lazed around on a vast plateau.

The winged serpent kept flying across the land, killing all that came in its path, with the humanoids following it like its humble servants.

Finally, it showed a battle between the serpent and a ridiculously gigantic bird-like creature. The snake won and once more soared into the sky as it grew larger and larger before finally morphing into a wyvern.

This wyvern then rampaged through the land, killing all it came across. An army of the same kind of bird it had killed earlier was consumed by a mist of poison that surrounded the scaled beast. It had no rival and slaughtered everything it encountered; not even its humanoid followers were spared from the onslaught.

At last, the wyvern found itself on a mountaintop, surrounded only by the desolate world below, a wasteland of its own creation. As it lay there, it roared toward the sky. The mural then displayed the passage of time, as the wyvern simply idled. No new grass or trees grew, no new life emerged. The land in which it had grown up was dead.

The wyvern stared toward the land it had created and finally found courage, no longer hesitating. It opened its wings and soared toward the heavens. The sky was shattered like it was made of glass, and a colossal explosion consumed the great wyvern.

The mural's final part was the once small snake emerging from the exploding planet, now no longer a wyvern, but a dragon. It soared upward into the stars as an entire universe opened up before it. Hunger was evident in its eyes.

After the images stopped, Jake stood in front of the mural for quite a while, just staring at it. It had shown the small mushroom-loving snake's complete evolutionary path, from a tiny creature to a dragon.

He marveled at the beautiful carving. The scene was frozen on the image of the wyvern breaking through the heavens.

He laid his hand on the mural as a warm glow entered him. At the same time, he heard the wall off to the side open up, showing the exit.

You have witnessed the will of a true dragon.

+10 Willpower

As the glow disappeared, he did not feel any different. His Willpower had always been his lowest stat, and now it had nearly doubled. He wasn't quite sure what the stat exactly did yet, but hey... Free stat points were free stat points. He decided to take a look at this status for the first time in quite a while.

```
Status
Name: Jake Thayne
Race: [Human(G) - lvl 4]
Class: [Archer - lvl 9]
Profession: N/A
Health Points (HP): 350/350
Mana Points (MP): 150/150
Stamina: 238/240
Stats
Strength: 24 (27)
Agility: 25 (30)
Endurance: 24
Vitality: 35
Toughness: 14
Wisdom: 15
Intelligence: 15
Perception: 43
Willpower: 23
Free Points: 3
```

He had experienced growth all over, especially in Strength and Agility with his new bracers. It appeared, however, that the stats weren't actually active here inside the dungeon.

The most pleasant surprise, however, was seeing his stamina refilled. When the system restored him, it hadn't only healed his injuries, but also fully renewed his resource pools. This meant he could keep going even without any potions or rest.

After closing his status menu again, he turned back to the mural, trying to imprint it on his mind. This was the path to power by an extraordinary being. He respected the snake, despite its ludicrous love of mushrooms.

Bowing toward the mural as a sign of recognition, he turned toward the exit, making his way forward. A reckless and insane desire entered his mind.

I would love to fight that dragon one day.

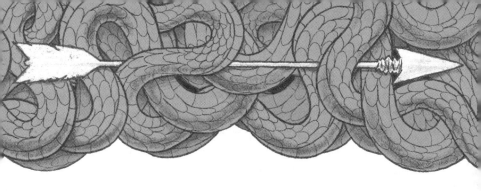

Chapter 21
An Impactful Choice

The next hallway was quite a bit longer than the previous one and suspiciously lacking in mushrooms. This meant that the narrow passage was entirely dark. Not that it mattered much to Jake with his sphere.

As he walked, he remembered that he had his skills back. He took out the dagger he had gotten during the second challenge room and identified it.

> [Dagger of Bloodletting (Common)] – A dagger created by an ancient, long-dead cult, made for sacrificial purposes. Enchantments: Any cuts made with this blade bleed more, for longer, and are harder to heal.

The enchantment explained why he'd bled so damn much when he cut himself. He put the dagger away as he proceeded down the hallway.

After walking for a couple of minutes, he turned a corner and saw a light source in the distance. This was not the blue light he had gotten used to, but "normal" light—the orange-whitish kind.

He sped up his walk and exited the hallway to find himself in a new room.

It was not what he expected. It looked like an old library or perhaps an office. There were bookshelves all along the walls, filled with old leather-bound books. A chair and a desk with a few writing utensils were positioned in the middle of the room.

There was also an old wooden door at the wall directly across from where he entered. As he hadn't seen any system messages yet, he walked up to one of the bookshelves and tried to take out a book, but was met with an invisible barrier of some sort.

He tried a couple of the other bookshelves with the same result. He also attempted to move some paper and the small cup filled with pencils and pens on the desk, both of which he couldn't touch due to the same kind of barrier. Finding nothing else of interest, he went through the only door in the room.

He was met with a small, relatively normal-looking hallway with five doors in it, two on each side of the corridor and one at the end. The first door he opened led into a room that had a bed in it. The rest of the room was absolutely barebones, with only a small wooden table and chair as well as a dresser and a closet. He was unable to open the dresser and closet, met with yet another invisible barrier.

Leaving the room, he closed the door after him and opened the next one. This one could only be described as a medieval bathroom that, for some reason, had a modern shower and toilet placed in it. He walked into the room and tried flushing the toilet, which surprisingly worked. So, an ancient, forgotten temple in a dungeon with running water. Got it.

The third room he entered was at the end of the hall, and what he found himself in wasn't exactly what one could call a "room." It was more like a hellscape in the form of a cave. Mushrooms. Everywhere. Not just the glowing blue kind, but also other less evil-looking ones.

The cave was not closed off either, and had another exit beside the wooden door. Jake walked out of the aforementioned exit and found himself in a small, walled-off garden. Flowers were growing everywhere, and weird-looking grass and bushes were aplenty, many of which he had seen before outside in the tutorial forest. There was even a small pond with different aquatic plants.

He called the garden walled off, but the wall that did so seemed to extend up into eternity. Hanging above the garden was a miniature version of the artificial sun he had seen outside in the forest, emitting both warmth and light. He was briefly confused, as Jake recalled it being late in the evening when he'd entered the Challenge Dungeon, and according to the timer counting down, only a couple of hours had passed since then.

Shaking his head at the weird garden, he went back through the cave and into the fourth room. This one was like an old laboratory. Not the modern kind, but the 1600s-mad-scientist kind. It looked like a dream come true for an insane chemist.

There were mortars and pestles, alembics, and a slew of other tools and materials. In the room were also open barrels with what seemed like water. Off to the side were closed cabinets that couldn't be opened either due to a barrier.

As he made his way out of the room toward the next, he wondered what exactly the system wanted him to do. No challenge had been presented, and no way forward had made itself known. This place seemed more like a living quarter than any kind of testing facility. *Maybe the challenge is to find the challenge?*

Opening the fifth door, he found himself within another hall like the ones in which he had done the challenges earlier. In the middle of the room was a pedestal. He moved to it and found a hand imprint on top of it. He looked at his hand and quickly connected the dots.

He put his hand on the imprint, and instantly, his danger sense flared as a black spike shot up, penetrating through it before he could react. He yelled out in pain and stumbled backward, and the room started rumbling.

A new platform had begun rising in front of the pedestal. Jake, however, barely registered this as he looked at the hole in his hand and saw small, subtle black lines spread through the veins in his hand. He suppressed his panic, rushing toward the newly risen platform. It didn't take a genius to figure out he had gotten poisoned.

On it was a book. The book was massive, far more massive than any book Jake had ever seen before. On the cover was the depiction of a small snake. The very same snake he had seen on the symbols and mural. He tried opening the book, and the system finally did something.

Dungeon Challenge: Become an Alchemist of the Malefic Viper and cure yourself of the poison running through your veins before it flares up and kills you. The poison will remain dormant for 30 days, not affecting the challenger in any way during the period.

Rejecting the profession will result in the challenger being fully restored and returned to the tutorial area. All rewards will be retained, and all items returned.

> **Cured yourself of poison 0/1**
>
> **Time remaining: 30 Days**
> **Become an Alchemist of the Malefic Viper?**
> **Y/N**

He was taken aback by the message. A profession? The N/A on his status page had annoyed him for a long time, but he hadn't expected to get one offered this way. It was the first option to obtain a profession he had seen since being introduced to the system, and he doubted it was an ordinary one. Alchemy, though? Not something he had any experience in at all outside of games.

He'd been rather good at the modern equivalent, chemistry, back in school, but he had never done it at any higher level. He also severely doubted that knowledge of chemical compounds would have a lot of use with magic being a thing and all.

The time limit was also thirty days. Looking at his just-impaled hand, it was rather obvious where the poison had come from. The wound had already scabbed over due to his high Vitality, and he didn't feel any different.

Jake also had the option of just quitting now and going back to the forest. It was the safe option for sure. He would be healed, walking away with a new dagger and a bonus to Willpower. Oh, and a bunch of shitty blue mushrooms, along with ten slightly nicer silver mushrooms.

It wasn't even like he had spent a lot of time getting everything.

But he was nothing if not someone who welcomed a challenge. He wanted a profession, and if this profession had any connection to that heaven-shattering dragon, it had to be powerful. Fantasy books and games had long conditioned him to unquestionably believe dragons to be apex creatures, after all.

Without further hesitation, he accepted the challenge.

> ***You have obtained the Alchemist of the Malefic Viper profession***

And with that message, everything went dark momentarily. Jake's head felt like it was split open as information surged into his mind, far more so than when he'd gotten his Archer class.

It was only for a few seconds, but it felt like hours before it finally stopped, leaving him with a massive headache and a considerable amount of system messages. He took a few more seconds to gather his thoughts as the headache faded away. When he felt better, he finally opened up the description of his new profession.

> **Alchemist of the Malefic Viper – The Alchemist of the Malefic Viper can combine natural treasures of the world to make potions and pills, transmute one material to another, and employ a slew of other mystical means to be discovered. This rare type of alchemist specializes in the concoction of poisons. From a craft classically bringing restoration and improvement, the Alchemist of the Malefic Viper brings pain, deterioration, and death. Stat bonuses per level: +2 Vit, +2 Wis, +1 Will, +1 Tough, +2 Free Points.**

The description of an alchemist was a lot like he had imagined. He had assumed the ability to make potions based on his experience playing certain online games during university. Transmutation was also a very classical trope of alchemists. *Perhaps I'll even make the Philosopher's Stone one day*, he joked to himself.

But that was where the familiarities ended. The latter part of the description suggested this variant of the alchemist profession focused on poison. The entire description was ominous, but then again, it was clearly modeled after, or at least heavily inspired by, a snake. To be more accurate, a small mushroom-eating snake. He assumed it to be the Malefic Viper.

The profession also provided more stat bonuses than his Archer class, giving 2 more stat points per level overall. None directly impacting combat, however, and he was slightly sad to see no bonus to Perception. But what was done was done; he had accepted it, and there was no going back.

He knew that the decision to pick the profession wasn't a minor one. Likely as significant as his class choice, if not more so, as this one was clearly not some basic profession handed out left and right. Finally... Jake had to admit that the thought of doing alchemy was kind of cool.

With that, he moved on to the next part: skills. With a quick skim, he saw that he had gained five and started going through them one by one.

> ***Gained skill***: [Herbology (Common)] – Grants knowledge of herbs found throughout the multiverse. The most numerous source of natural treasures comes in the form of herbs found throughout existence. The knowledge of plants and their effects is, therefore, essential to any alchemist. An alchemist must know what he works with in order to create his products, after all. Grants the ability to recognize herbs at a glance, and correctly identify their properties.

A relatively self-explanatory skill, and one of the reasons for the sudden influx of information he'd gotten upon receiving the profession. He now knew of a lot of different plants he previously had no idea existed. It was scary that the system could directly implant knowledge in one's head.

The way the knowledge worked was weird. It was not immediate knowledge, like how he'd known how to use his bow from previous training. It was the kind of knowledge that felt like it gradually appeared if he thought of something relevant to the skill. Like if he thought of needing a plant that had healing properties, a considerable number of potential herbs suddenly came to mind.

Shaking his head at the frankly disturbing phenomenon, he moved on.

Gained skill: [Brew Potion (Common)] – Potion brewing is the bread and butter of most alchemists. A potion can be the savior in a time of need, or that extra boost to defeat your opponent. Allows for the brewing of potions with common rarity and below. Must have suitable materials and equipment in order to create potions. Adds a minor increase to the effectiveness of created potions based on Wisdom.

Gained skill: [Concoct Poison (Common)] – While most focus on the aspect of giving life through their craft, others prefer to take it away. Allows for the concoction of common-rarity poisons and below. Must have suitable materials and equipment in order to create poisons. Adds a minor increase to the effectiveness of created poisons based on Wisdom.

These two skills were incredibly similar in design, but very different when it came to the results. It also didn't come with a lot of implanted knowledge. He had some new understandings of how to use the tools he'd found in the laboratory earlier, but they in no way felt familiar. It was more like he had watched a tutorial video online, introducing him to the very basics of making potions and poisons.

Thinking back on his talks with Casper, who had gotten the Basic Archery skill without any previous experience ever using a bow, he had told Jake about something similar. He knew how to hold a bow and fire an arrow, but nothing further than that. Despite him and Jake both having the same skill, and at the same rarity, Jake was vastly superior in his ability to use it.

He got an upgrade in rarity for the skill after recalling his training, but the rank-up did not come with any knowledge.

The only difference between skills seemed to be the rarity. With no skill levels existing, Jake had a theory that skills' effectiveness were purely up to the wielder of said skills. Perhaps some kind of line existed where skills would get a rarity upgrade based on how good he was, but he doubted it would be that simple. Take the archery skill as an example.

Jake was a somewhat experienced archer. Theoretically, his knowledge of how to wield a bow was close to the level of an athlete. Maybe even higher, as he had put a lot of time into looking things up himself instead of having a trainer do such things for him. And yet he only had archery at common rarity. Something else must be required to upgrade to higher ranks. Maybe it just took time, or perhaps some qualitative threshold had to be reached.

In other words, a skill granted basic instinctual proficiency in using it, but anything more than that would have to be learned. And if you wanted the skill to get better, you would have to work on improving it. That was at least what Jake believed, based on the evidence so far.

Having no way to either confirm or disprove his hypothesis, he moved on to the last two skills.

> *Gained skill*: [Toxicology (Uncommon)] – The knowledge of all that is toxic. Be able to recognize poisonous substances at a glance and correctly identify their properties. To concoct the deadliest toxins, one must know what to mix, after all.

This one was exactly the same as the Herbology skill, just with toxic materials and uncommon instead of common rarity. It was not limited to herbs, however. As an example, if he thought about the water that had nearly killed him earlier, he now knew that said water was some kind of toxic liquid with necrotic properties. He didn't know the details of the water, just the basics of what it was.

Moving on to the last skill, he was pleasantly surprised to see the "rare" rarity tag.

> *Gained skill*: [Malefic Viper's Poison (Rare)] – The Malefic Viper stalks its prey and needs only to strike once as venom devours its prey. Increases the potency of all crafted poisons.
> Grants the ability to craft a poison with a rarity above that of your Concoct Poison skill if certain conditions are met. The poison may at most be upgraded to the rarity of the Malefic Viper's Poison skill (Common --> Rare). Allows poison not to lose efficacy for a short amount of time after being applied to a weapon.

This skill was the namesake of the entire profession, he assumed. More potent poisons and a chance to craft poisons with a higher rarity both seemed okay, though he had nothing to compare it to. The last effect was especially interesting to him, however.

This skill opened the possibility to use his profession more actively in combat. What could be more dangerous than an arrow to the face? A poisoned arrow to the face.

He had one more notification remaining, which was another pleasant surprise.

> *Skill Upgraded*: [Identify (Inferior -->
> Common)] - Identification skill, known by
> all but the smallest of children of the myriad
> races. The skill allows you to attempt to
> identify any object or creature you are
> focusing on.

The only difference in the skills description was the "basic" being removed, so it now just called it an "identification skill." Not much to see there, really. But Jake was still kind of excited to see what he could now Identify. Perhaps he could even Identify other humans?

He guessed the upgrade had something to do with having both a profession and a class, or maybe it was due to the two skills, Herbology and Toxicology, giving him more knowledge. Looking back, both of those skills included a sentence about being able to Identify herbs and toxins.

Closing all his windows, he looked down at his hand, which was still healing. After scanning the room once more and finding nothing of interest, he turned around and headed straight for the garden area to test his new skills.

Chapter 22
Alchemy!

Jake entered the cave, looking around at all the different fungi and moss, deciding to Identify the infamous blue mushrooms first. When he did it before, he'd just gotten a message saying [Mushroom], so he kind of expected more. Which it delivered.

[Bluebright Mushroom (Common)] – A poisonous blue mushroom that emits blue light. While it is not poisonous to touch, the juices found within are highly toxic. Often used for lighting due to it only requiring mana to sustain itself.

Knowing the name of the blue menace did not alleviate his distaste for the evil fungus. It was good to see that they were only poisonous if squeezed or eaten, though. His next target was another type of mushroom, this one rather plain-looking.

[Flytrap Mushroom (Inferior)] – A carnivorous and poisonous mushroom that eats insects to accelerate its growth.

This one was a lower rarity, but still poisonous. Jake looked around a bit more, finding quite a few different kinds of mushrooms, nearly all of them inferior rarity.

Shifting his focus to the green moss growing everywhere on the walls, he used Identify once more.

> [Green Moss (Inferior)] – A widespread kind of moss, found in places with little or no sunlight and adequate mana saturation. A typical ingredient in potions and poisons alike.

So, jack-of-all-trades moss. Jake then noticed a patch of moss that was darker than the rest, so he also Identified that.

> [Aged Green Moss (Common)] - A widespread kind of moss, found in places with little or no sunlight and adequate mana saturation. A typical ingredient in potions and poisons alike. This moss has been thoroughly soaked in mana over time.

Common-rarity moss. Did this mean that age was a factor when it came to the rarity of plants?

Finding nothing more of particular interest in the cave, he exited to the garden. The first thing he did here was Identify the grass. He once more noticed some off-color patches spread throughout.

> [Evergreen Grass (Inferior)] – A widespread herb found throughout the multiverse in any place with adequate nature–affinity mana. While the grass only offers minor restorative effects, it is a great catalyst when mixed with other herbs.

[Aged Evergreen Grass (Common)] A widespread herb found throughout the multiverse in any place with adequate nature-affinity mana. While the grass only offers minor restorative effects, it is a great catalyst when mixed with other herbs. This grass has aged and absorbed more mana than most Evergreen Grass.

It was the same concept as the moss in the cave. Recalling some of the knowledge given by the system, he knew that the moss was often used when concocting poisons, while the grass was used when making potions.

Many flowers were also spread throughout the garden, the most abundant kind being four lavender types: a blue one, a red one, a green one, and, in between the small patches of these flowers, a rainbow-colored type, which looked very fantasy-like. Once more, Jake identified all the plants.

[Blue Lavender (Inferior)] – A very abundant herb found nearly everywhere with any kind of mana. Mana is stored in the small flowers growing on the stalk, with the stem itself containing the useful juices. Known as the main ingredient of mana potions.

[Red Lavender (Inferior)] – A very abundant herb found nearly everywhere with any kind of mana. Mana is stored in the small flowers growing on the stalk, with the stem itself containing the useful juices. Known as the main ingredient of health potions.

[Green Lavender (Inferior)] – A very abundant herb found nearly everywhere with any kind of mana. Mana is stored in the small flowers

> growing on the stalk, with the stem itself containing the useful juices. Known as the main ingredient of stamina potions.
>
> [Rainbow Lavender (Common)] – A relatively abundant herb found nearly everywhere with any kind of mana, usually surrounded by its lesser variants. Mana is stored in the small flowers growing on the stalk, with the stem itself containing the useful juices. Known as the main ingredient of rejuvenation potions.

These flowers straight-up informed him that they were the main ingredients in potions. And he had a very, *very* strong feeling that he would come to craft a lot of potions.

More flowers were present in the garden, some of them not even returning anything when he identified them and others being only inferior rarity. Lastly, he went to the small pond and surprisingly successfully identified the water.

> [Purified Water] – Pure water, free of any kind of contamination. Great for mixing potions and poisons alike.

And with that, he had everything he needed to start making stuff. At least he assumed he did. The only way to find out was to test it out. What could possibly go wrong, mixing a bunch of unknown substances in an old temple left by a cult-worshipping a possibly long-dead snake?

Jake began picking up plants, but only the inferior-rarity ones, as he assumed they would be the easiest to experiment with. Opening his satchel to put in some of the lavender flowers, he spotted the ten silver mushrooms he had picked up during his very first challenge in this dungeon.

He had to admit that he had kind of forgotten those. Without any expectations, he decided to Identify one of them and was taken aback by the result.

> [Argentum Vitae Mushroom (Rare)] – A silver mushroom only grown in places with extremely high mana density. The mushroom has a solid exterior that, if broken, reveals the actual mushroom within. This type of mushroom's juices usually are highly poisonous, but this mushroom has evolved to bring life instead. +1 Vitality upon consumption.

He took a deep breath after reading the description. These were 10 Free Points to Vitality, 11 factoring in his Bloodline Patriarch title, giving a 10% bonus.

He was just about to eat one when he stopped himself. These mushrooms were still raw. What if he could get more than a single Vitality per mushroom?

There was also that whole thing with a poison in his body that would flare up and kill him in a month. He would not find it unfitting for these mushrooms to somehow be needed not to die. Thus he decided to leave them be for now and instead continued collecting more ingredients.

Leaving the garden through the cave, he also collected a stack of mushrooms, heading straight for the laboratory.

He went through the lab once more, this time being able to open the cabinets and interact with all the equipment. The cabinets were all filled with small glass bottles, and the water in the barrels was the same pure water found in the small pond.

Jake had initially planned on starting to make something right away, but quickly hit his first roadblock. He had no idea how to. He had been given some incredibly basic knowledge, but nothing that would allow him actually to make something. In fact, the few fragments of knowledge he did have only served to inform him that he didn't know enough.

Each plant had requirements for how to handle it properly, and each potion or poison their own recipe. None of this was given to him for free, which led him to the other room previously covered in barriers.

In the library/office he had first arrived in, he could now touch all of the many bookshelves. Oh, and on a side note, the door through which he had initially entered was gone, so going back to the prior challenge rooms wasn't an option.

Not that he had any intention of leaving. Walking up to one of the bookshelves, he took a random book out, and the first thing he noticed was that it was clearly written in English.

Which was quite impressive, considering that he was multilingual, and yet it had chosen English. *What if I wanted it to be... Oh, now it is.* Before his eyes, the entire text had now changed languages. He couldn't help but try it again, and found that it switched back and forth with only a thought.

Jake found it quite humorous to experiment with, but sadly, he couldn't play around forever. Ultimately, what language it was in was meaningless, all that mattered was that he could easily read and understand every word. So he began to actually read what was written.

The first book seemed to be some kind of history book, detailing the history of alchemy. While it was interesting and very enlightening, it wasn't what he was looking for. He quickly discarded it and started reading the covers of some of the different books, going from top to bottom on the bookshelf. He quickly located the first one he wanted—a book detailing the creation of inferior-rarity health potions.

After looking a bit more, he ended up having six books stacked on the desk, including **Alchemy for Novices, Volume 1; Alchemy for Novices, Volume 2;** and **An Introduction to Potions: The Health Potion.** He also had books of the same series for mana and stamina potions, and the last book was **Poisons: The Elementary.**

The three potions books were pretty short and had a plethora of pictures and diagrams of different herbs, most of them recognizable to him. The Alchemy for Novices volumes were massive tomes and contained many diagrams and step-by-step guides too, but most of it was just a buttload of text.

The most comprehensive book was the one on poisons, and the one he had decided to save for last.

Checking the timer, he had spent around a few hours since he had gotten his profession. Having no time to waste, he started reading the first volume on novice alchemy.

The first thing he noticed was how fast it went. He was already an experienced reader, having finished university and being used to reading a lot. But this was at an entirely different level. It took him only an hour to go through the first hundred pages. And that was with the pens and papers placed on the desk being used avidly in making bookmarks and taking down notes.

The whole thing brought Jake back to his university days. The only thing he really lacked was some hot tea and some good music.

The content of the book was exactly as the cover said. It introduced alchemy. It had small parts on transmutation and pill-making, and even some details reminding Jake of more modern chemical theories. Still, the main content was detailing the process of making potions using herbs.

It went into how to process the herbs, the tools often used when doing so, what type of water was suitable for different kinds of potions, how to properly store and prepare the herbs, et cetera. The knowledge on concocting poisons was somewhat limited, and pretty much only focused on how to avoid introducing poison into your creations.

After another couple of hours of reading, he wanted to give it a shot. Was he ready? Probably not, but he felt like at least trying. Jake got up and stretched before walking toward the laboratory. He had left his satchel back in the lab, as he saw no reason to carry it around.

He had learned a lot from his reading, one of those things being how stupid it was just to pluck a bunch of herbs and throw them together in a big bundle in the satchel. At least he had not been dumb enough to also throw in moss and fungi.

After a bit of salvaging, most of the herbs were still useful. Jake had brought along with him some of the books and his notes. Without further ado, he started meticulously following them on how to create potions.

He ground the grass into a paste, mixed it with water, and injected mana into a small, enchanted burner to boil the purified water. Rather than university, where it had been all reading and numbers, this felt more like chemistry. Far more practical.

Potions for health and mana were not made one by one. Not the lower-rarity ones, at least. You usually made batches that could vary quite a bit based on how well you did. The mix could quickly become too weak or too strong, resulting in adverse effects; the system recognized them as failed creations.

Mana also played a massive role in alchemy. The bowl in which one mixed the batch required mana to be injected, thus entering through it. The same held true for the mortar and pestle, the pestle itself being enchanted to accept mana being channeled through it.

All the equipment used to craft was enchanted with practical things. Self-Repair was found on practically everything, and Jake had already found out from his cloak and bracers that Self-Repair also came with a self-cleaning functionality.

His first batch was an attempt to make mana potions, the least complex of the three types. It turned into a not-quite-blue mixture that smelled terrible. Luckily, the lab also came with a sink that had a faucet, and all that one would expect. Sadly, the water coming out was not classified as purified, so he had to keep getting water from the pond.

A lot of information was found within the different books; most interesting was a section on stats. It even helped explain the effects of them, more so than Jake had been able to deduce himself so far. It has to be mentioned that the information was heavily limited, almost like the system had censored some things.

As for stats that were good for alchemy, Wisdom was mentioned as the overall most important. It increased total mana and the ability to retain knowledge of recipes and such. The fact that both poisons' and potions' effectiveness was increased by Wisdom also played a considerable part without a doubt. The second-most important was Willpower, as it increased mana regeneration, something that was new knowledge to Jake.

Willpower also helped with focusing while doing alchemy, though the book mentioned that no amount of stats could make up for the lack of personal perseverance.

It clearly looked like the book should have more info than that, but a considerable part had been cut out.

While this was a mystery for sure, there was one that irked him even more. Why did his profession increase Vitality by 2 and Toughness by 1 too? However, that was a mystery quickly solved as he briefly skimmed the small section on stats in the book on poisons.

Concocting poisons, compared to nearly every other aspect of alchemy, was no safe practice. The fumes alone could kill most, and just being close to poison daily came with many dangers. On top of that, those dabbling in poison also sometimes used their own bodies to test their newest concoctions, the occasional alchemist even going so far as to cultivate toxins within their own body.

Therefore, the book said that one should not dabble in poison before one had sufficient Vitality and serviceable Toughness. The book also mentioned that most alchemy professions did not increase Vitality or Toughness, so investing Free Points in those stats was recommended if one wished to pursue concocting poisons as a specialty—a recommendation Jake could quite easily ignore, as he had plenty.

After emptying the mixing bowl and cleaning it, he tried mixing another batch of mana potions. He used the entire blue lavender flower, grinding up the stalk and flower and mixing it with the evergreen grass.

Going through the motions once more ended in another failure. Injecting mana was not as simple as just channeling it like it was with the quiver; instead, one had to do it carefully. The injection part was where the difference between a skilled alchemist and a novice was found.

He had to somehow control the mana he injected into it, guide the entire process with his mana. Luckily, it didn't require much to make the most basic mana potions, but it was still a challenge. The books had detailed how to do it, but a lot of it was still touch-and-go.

After making another four failed batches, he still had sufficient mana but was out of ingredients. After another roundtrip to the garden, he had enough for another crafting session.

He continued trying, making batch after batch, as he wrote down notes on why he'd failed and what to improve. Slowly, he felt the improvements. His last attempt turned out to closely resemble a mana potion but wasn't quite there yet. By that point, he had been at it for nearly twelve hours and was exhausted both mentally and physically. His stamina was still high, but he could barely focus.

Going to the room with the bed, he quickly took a look in the closet and dresser, finding clothes in both. They looked rather simple, but it was good to have something to change into. His old clothes beneath his cloak were well and truly battered by now, and, if he had to be honest, smelled a bit.

But quite frankly, Jake was too tired to further think of it as he collapsed on the bed and fell asleep.

Waking up, he felt wholly rejuvenated but panicked slightly as he checked the timer. He let out a sigh of relief upon realizing he had only slept for a bit over five hours. His stamina was topped off, while his mana was at 70%—more than enough for another good round of alchemy.

Feeling refreshed and sharp, he went to the laboratory once more after a quick shower and change of clothes. He briefly skimmed over his notes and got to work. The part where he had to prepare the ingredients he had down to a T. His timing of adding ingredients to the mix was also adequate.

No, the final hurdle was the mana injection. It wouldn't be an understatement to say that it was 90% of the process.

One had plenty of leeway making mana potions when it came to temperature control, so once everything was in the mix and one had to combine ingredients into an actual potion, it was just pure mana control.

And now, with a clear head, Jake felt sharper than ever. He knew what to do and how to do it. He just had to execute. The mana poured gently into the mixture as he controlled it with the help of the intricate runes inscribed on the mixing bowl. One very much had to go by feel, and this time, Jake felt like all was as it should be.

A short while later, a refreshing smell permeated the laboratory as he turned off the fire, a beautiful blue mixture in his bowl. He knew he had succeeded, and the system message shortly after only confirmed it as he smiled to himself.

*You have successfully crafted [Mana Potion (Inferior)] – A new kind of creation has been made. Bonus experience earned *
'DING!' Profession: [Alchemist of the Malefic Viper] has reached level 1 - Stat points allocated, +2 Free Points
'DING!' Race: [Human (G)] has reached level 5 - Stat points allocated, +1 Free Point

Chapter 23
Progression

Feeling the warm glow run through his body from the level-ups was as comfortable as ever. He was equally as pleased to see that profession experience also helped with his race level.

Looking at his stats, he noticed that he now had 6 unspent Free Points. Jake still felt very unsure of how to distribute them best. Was there some way to make an optimal build? Ultimately, he decided this wasn't the time to try and meta-game the system. You know, with his life on the line and all that.

So, having decided not to hoard the points any longer, he threw them in the stat best for alchemy according to all the books: Wisdom. He felt the warm glow once more before opening his status menu to confirm the changes.

Status
Name: Jake Thayne
Race: [Human (G) – lvl 5]
Class: [Archer – lvl 9]
Profession: [Alchemist of the Malefic Viper – lvl 1]
Health Points (HP): 380/380

```
Mana Points (MP): 192/240
Stamina: 235/250
Stats
Strength: 28
Agility: 31
Endurance: 25
Vitality: 38
Toughness: 16
Wisdom: 24
Intelligence: 16
Perception: 44
Willpower: 25
Free Points: 0
```

Not much had changed with his stats besides Wisdom getting a considerable bump upwards from the levels and Free Points. Nodding to himself, he closed the menu once more and turned his attention to the mixing bowl in front of him.

Looking at the completed batch of mana potions, he felt very satisfied with himself. Walking to the cabinet, he took out a handful of bottles and began putting the concoction into them. The bottles were perfectly sized to get the full benefit one could from each potion.

Jake had wondered what would happen if one drank an additional potion during the cooldown period. He and his colleagues had some theories, most of them determining it would end badly if one drank more than two within an hour.

But now he knew what would happen. And it was a big shocker. If one consumed two potions within an hour, the second could cause horrific consequences, such as being slightly less thirsty or having one less potion to drink.

Jokes aside, one could pour down mana potions for days without suffering any adverse consequences. It was basically just water. Of course, this raised countless more questions as to where the excess energy would go.

It was honestly frustrating how none of the books even bothered to talk about it. They essentially said: "So yeah, the second one doesn't work because that's how it is."

AKA, system-fuckery was how potions worked. The batch he had just made could be consumed as is, but would only have the effect of the single potion, so one was more or less forced to bottle it up. It also wouldn't register as an actual item before being in a bottle or another similar type of container.

Moving on back to the present, Jake ended up with a total of only three bottles, something that, according to the books, was considered quite terrible. Not that Jake cared much; he was just proud of his accomplishment.

Using Identify on the potion, it only echoed how terrible they were.

> **[Mana Potion (Inferior)] – Restores 87 mana when consumed.**

He remembered Caroline telling him that the mana potions that the system had given them upon entering the tutorial had given her at least 130 mana. He would have to thank Jacob for being terrible enough at combat the next time they met.

The fact that Jake could see the exact amount restored was also something new. He was unsure if it was due to Identify going up in rank or a bonus from one of the new profession skills. Or perhaps it was the presence of the profession itself.

Jake put the potions on one of the other tables in the laboratory with a smile. He planned on drinking them later, but he still had enough mana not to make full use of them. Having proven himself able to make something, he started mixing a second batch after cleaning up a bit.

However, his festive mood quickly died down as he failed the next two batches. Still, it was rapidly alleviated when the third batch of mana potions succeeded—another three potions, with exactly the same properties.

Seeing his mana had gotten a little low, he drank one of the potions he had made and felt his mana fill up to nearly full once more. He planned on drinking a potion every hour with the internal cooldown to keep working, with the only limit being his mental energy.

The mixing continued. A day and over a dozen mana potions consumed later, he finally started to get exhausted once more, and his last two batches had failed due to him not being able to focus.

It was hard work, but the results spoke for themselves:

> *'DING!' Profession: [Alchemist of the Malefic Viper] has reached level 2 - Stat points allocated, +2 Free Points*
>
> *'DING!' Profession: [Alchemist of the Malefic Viper] has reached level 3 - Stat points allocated, +2 Free Points*
>
> *'DING!' Race: [Human (G)] has reached level 6 - Stat points allocated, +1 Free Point*
>
> *'DING!' Profession: [Alchemist of the Malefic Viper] has reached level 4 - Stat points allocated, +2 Free Points*

The levels were impressive, but it was, without a doubt, slower than leveling his class. He had spent more than twenty-four hours on the challenge already, and yet he was only level 4 in the profession. Compared to outside, where he—in less time than that—had reached level 9. If he had been more efficient and gone solo earlier, he would, without a doubt, be well into the double digits by now.

Looking at the dungeon challenge window, he noted the time.

> **Time remaining: 28 Days – 22:53:11**

Walking back to the bed once more, he brought the book on health potions along for a quick read before taking another nap. He had decided to try and make them the next day, as the mana potion's experience had started going down and also because he had enough of them to keep himself going for a while.

Health potions were, according to the *Alchemy for Novices* book, the second easiest type of potion to make, just after the mana one. The process was very similar, with only slight variations. The pattern and method of injecting mana into the mixture was the most significant difference, and quite a lot harder than with mana potions.

Mana potions were quite natural to make. You did not need to change the properties of the mana injected; you just had to purify and inject it. With health potions, you had to change the nature of the mana. Ultimately, the potion was still a kind of condensed energy close to mana, and Jake had no proper understanding of how exactly it all worked, so he just left that up to the system.

He also wanted to start making poisons soon, but he felt it would be slightly more challenging than the three basic resource-restoration potions. The books agreed with his intuition. From what he had briefly read, concocting poisons had many of the same methods as potions, so there was a lot of overlap. Hence, it wasn't like his practice on potions was wasted.

In the end, concocting poisons was also primarily about injecting mana properly and controlling the crafting process.

After reading the book on health potions, Jake put it on the floor as there was no bedtable. Seconds after closing his eyes, he fell asleep. He dreamed of potions and alchemy, genuinely looking forward to waking up and continuing.

Jacob, Caroline, Bertram, Casper, Ahmed, and Theodore were all walking with a group of Richard's men as they hunted once more. The team they went with was the usual, except for Caroline, who could join them while Richard took a rest back at camp.

Richard had reached level 12 earlier that day and had gotten a new ability at level 10 that allowed him to bash with his shield and send out a shockwave, knocking down anyone in its path. With it and his increased stats, he had hunted many beasts over level 10, and they had even relocated their base once to get further into the forest and find stronger enemies to hunt.

The only one from their original group at level 10 was Caroline, who often went with Richard and his so-called "elite squad." Caroline had, at level 10, learned a ranged version of her heal, much to the delight of everyone.

The entire camp had also expanded significantly. When they had joined, Richard's group had consisted of twenty-six people excluding them. Well, twenty people with the six that Jake had killed. After joining, they'd shot up to twenty-nine, and after recruiting some more, the group was now a bit over fifty. Richard was still in charge, of course.

They had gotten one more healer, but he was only level 6, and Caroline had shown herself to be competent, so Richard kept her around in his squad. The passive regeneration aura alone was enough to keep a healer around initially. In combat, they often contributed little to nothing, as their healing was touch-based, but with her now being able to heal from a distance, her worth shot up significantly.

Jacob was the leader of this small group that usually had to go without a healer. He was level 8, and the only one in their squad who was level 9, besides Caroline, was Casper. Dennis and Lina were both in another team. Jacob knew that this was due to Richard not wanting their group to all be together, even if one considered Joanna, who was stuck back in the camp.

Speaking of Joanna, she had brought with her a pleasant surprise. She had started fixing up cloaks and robes for people and conjuring arrows for the archers after joining, trying to make herself useful. A couple of hours ago, just before they left the camp, Joanna had unlocked a profession.

This was the first instance of anyone obtaining a profession that they knew of. Joanna had been into stitching and sewing before the tutorial, which had likely helped her unlock it to begin with. This was only a theory, though.

According to Joanna, the profession didn't give many stat points per level, hers only offering 1 Wisdom, 1 Willpower, 1 Agility, and 1 Free Point per level.

Seeing that the stat gains were so low compared to the time investment, Richard's interest significantly waned.

Until Joanna got to level 1 in the profession, that is, and as she was also level 3 in her class, she leveled her race too. This instantly reignited his interest. Every single race level gave +1 to all stats and an extra Free Point, making them even more valuable than both class and profession.

His interest was further amplified after he experienced that leveling only got harder and harder, and level 10 seemed to be one of those difficulty jumps. Hunting with a team also hurt his experience gain, but as he was more powerful in a group due to his class's nature, he had to be in one.

Making their way back to base, Jacob thought about what Jake was up to. It had been close to two days since he left, and they had neither seen nor heard anything from him. He and Richard had a tacit understanding never to mention him, but Jacob still wondered.

He was not afraid for Jake's well-being, more so curious as to what level he had reached by now. Okay, he was a bit worried, but the guy could clearly handle himself. At least he hoped he could, as Jacob had encountered some nasty things.

After a final fight with a small group of badgers, one of them being above level 10, they finally made it back. Speaking of the badgers, those things turned out to get a lot more dangerous when they reached the double digits. Not only because of their size, but because of the venom their claws now secreted.

If Caroline had not been in the group, they would not even have tried fighting it. Another group had lost two people to one of the beasts, as they got severely poisoned from just a few minor scratches. The potions they drank only functioned to extend the suffering as they died. The importance of a healer was once again evident.

Back in camp, Jacob went straight to Richard, reporting how their little hunt went.

"Jacob, welcome back," the huge man said. "Any difficulties?"

His shield was leaning on a stone next to him. It was not the one a heavy warrior started with, but a far larger tower shield. He had gotten it earlier that day, and it was, according to Caroline, an uncommon-rarity item.

"No, nothing special. It's getting harder and harder to find enough beasts to hunt, and those we do tend to be on the weaker side. Should we consider moving further into the forest?" Jacob took a seat on a stone across from Richard.

It was frustrating trying to level up at any decent pace. Whenever the group moved, Richard would have the light warriors and archers with stealth scout the area, and he would monopolize any strong beasts with his own squad.

"I guess we should," Richard said. "Double digits are getting scarce. Did you find any items or tokens while out?"

Another one of Richard's rules. All items had to be given to him, so they could be given out to those who could make the best use of them. Which is to say, every item was monopolized by Richard and his buddies. Richard had already known of items the day they joined, and it did make Jacob a bit sour that they might have missed some as they made their initial trek in the forest.

He didn't doubt that many just kept them to themselves. It was risky, as Jacob didn't want to learn the consequences of being found out, but he understood why some did it anyway. Jacob didn't hide them, though. He was playing the long game.

"Yes, Casper found a single common-rarity upgrade token," he said, giving it to Richard. "I think the number of boxes in the area are also getting scarce."

"Casper is the archer, right?" Richard asked, to which Jacob nodded. "He is getting close to level 10 already, right? Tell him to keep up the good work; a spot in the elite team may just open up. We're also getting some new members soon, so it may be necessary to have him help lead them."

"I'll be sure to tell him," Jacob answered, hiding his contempt.

Yet another one of Richard's tactics. If a squad besides his own had anyone who stood out, he would try to separate them. He was not open about it and often backed his choices with sound logic, but Jacob had been in management long enough to recognize nefarious leadership like that.

Richard was actively trying to limit cohesion. He allowed enough for them to get used to each other and to be able to work together, but anything more than that he wanted to avoid. Jacob and his colleagues' position was quite unusual as they had all known each other before the tutorial. Richard and his gang of people was the only other group like theirs.

Most groups of ten that had entered the tutorial were strangers. Random crowds of people being thrown together. Since the system had taken people close to each other physically as it transported them, at least to some extent, it did mean that many had ended up entering with at least one or two people they knew, though.

But Richard broke those small groups up whenever he could. He had a million excuses as to why it was for the best, but people mostly just did as he said out of fear. Not necessarily fear of being attacked, but also fear of being tossed out of the camp.

While the way stuff was run was far from ideal, it was far safer than likely anywhere else. One had to remember that not everyone was fit for combat or willing to risk their own lives. Many that joined simply huddled up in the camp. At least Joanna had now opened a path for them to progress without any need to face beasts.

As Jacob walked back to his colleagues, a young man wearing a robe—one that had clearly been upgraded with a token—walked by. The wand at his hip was another either upgraded or looted item. It instantly gave away his identity as a caster. The man, who was barely even a man at all, was in his late teens and wore a big stupid smile on his face.

Jacob remembered that his name was William, and he had joined after Jacob and his group. Richard knew little of this young man, only that he was clearly competent and had reached above level 10 before he even joined them. He had not been with any group when he joined, but had come alone.

His story was that strong monsters had ambushed them shortly after entering the tutorial, and he'd gotten away as the only survivor. Yeah, no one was buying that, but as they couldn't prove him wrong, they just rolled with it. The predominant theory was that he had run away.

Most surprising, however, was the young man still insisting on hunting alone even after joining. Richard had initially wanted him in the elite squad but was declined. He had considered merely "removing" the man permanently but had decided against it. Jacob had become privy to this information through Caroline, who had shared most with him in the beginning, but it had gotten far worse recently as she began keeping more secrets.

Jacob understood why he had not done anything, though. Richard could not do it openly after all, as it would be bad for morale, and Richard perhaps feared a repeat of Jake, who had killed his right-hand man and five others. The only survivor, a mess, had still not left the camp since he returned. So, sending a group covertly after the caster was a risk. One he seemed unwilling to take.

Instead, he appeared to go with the principle of keeping his potential enemies close. Jacob decided to not head back just yet, but stayed close to hear the caster and Richard talk.

"I heard you talk to that guy," William said to Richard. "I also think we should move further in. Nothing gives any experience points around here anymore." He sighed before continuing. "I'm afraid that boredom will end up killing me before any of those 'roided-out animals do."

"I hear you; I plan on moving when the last group returns," Richard answered, clearly a bit annoyed at the teenager's flippant attitude to the whole tutorial.

"Great!" the caster answered with a smile. "Oh, by the way, I need more mana potions. Got any?"

"Go ask some of the others," Richard answered, trying, but failing, to hide his annoyance. Jacob had heard William had already taken nearly all of their spare mana potions, and Richard only had the ones he purposely kept hidden away—another open secret, that one. Richard likely wanted to save some for the healers in case of an emergency.

"Oh, okay," William answered as he turned around, happily walking toward the campfire where people were doing various tasks. Some were stitching, others trying to make something out of the leather, and there was even a guy trying to draw with some charcoal from the fire—all of them attempting to unlock professions.

As William walked away from Richard, he thought to himself how great this place was. He was finally free, his mind unshackled. Purified from all that had suppressed him in the old world.

He had returned to perfection.

TO BE CONTINUED IN

THE PRIMAL HUNTER

VOLUME 2